The Fairytales of Lightfall Hollow

The Fairytales of Lightfall Hollow

Susan C. Ramirez

Illustrations by Kathy Hebner

Illustrations by Kathy Hebner

Manuscript Format by Daria Lacy

Published by Mountain Laurel Press

P.O. Box 117

Schellsburg, PA 15559

www.susancramirez.com

This book was produced with editorial guidance and technical support from **Self-Publishing Consultant Robin Moore**. To learn more about gaining assistance on the pathway to publishing before a world-wide readership, visit:
www.robin-moore.com

CONTENTS

Because of You

And All Children Everywhere

Whatever Your Age

"Life itself is the most wonderful fairy tale."
Hans Christian Anderson

Chapter One

The Hollow

 HE FIRST fairy I ever met was Luna Shadow. That was many years ago when I was a little girl. Since then, I have met countless more fairies and other magical creatures. They are my friends. Together we share a wonderful life in Lightfall Hollow.

Lightfall Hollow is a small woodland valley cradled in the Allegheny Mountains of Pennsylvania. The first time I saw the hollow, it was my father's hunting ground, a wilderness he had known and loved since boyhood, inherited from his grandmother a decade before. Although I was only three years old, I vividly remember riding through its forest on my father's shoulders. What I saw was an enchanted land. Like Daddy, I was wonderstruck.

For a hunting camp, my father had torn down a log barn from

pioneer days and rebuilt it as a one-room cabin. It was crude, dank, dark, and drafty, and the roof leaked. I often got splinters from its rough wooden floor and walls. There was no electricity or running water. A pot-bellied stove provided heat. Windows of cracked and wavy glass provided the only air conditioning. They were almost impossible to open and stuck when they did. Water came from buckets filled and hand-carried from a spring dribbling out of the ground a quarter mile away. The bathroom, which was more than one hundred feet from the cabin, was a gag-producing outhouse.

It was also stinky inside the cabin. This was partially because of the long, musty flannel curtains printed with humorous deer hunting scenes that divided the cabin in two. In front of the curtains was the living, cooking, and dining area. Behind the curtains were the sleeping accommodations, two massive and tall bunk beds my father had made. Each bed was a double. The lower bunks took up almost the entire floor space, and the top bunks, which were each reached by climbing a rickety ladder, were dangerously close to the ceiling. Even as a little girl, I sometimes hit my head.

To top off the primitive decor, as well as to add to the bad odor, hanging on the wall above a curtainless window and between the two bunk beds was an old, rank, taxidermied moose head named George. There was nothing outwardly appealing about George. He had a crooked nose, broken antlers that turned down, cloudy glass eyeballs, and tattered, lopsided ears. Moths had long feasted upon his hide, leaving little holes and large bald spots, and his beard had been stolen by mice for their nests. What fur remained was dingy in color, covered in ancient grime, sprinkled with George's own spilled sawdust stuffing, and blotched with a gray mold that made him smell like wet socks.

Despite his shabby looks and offensive reek, I was very fond of George. Mostly because of the make-believe, yet somehow convincing bedtime stories my father told about the moose and his sensational adventures. Always at the end of his latest tall tale, Daddy would blow me a kiss, and I would fly off to dreamland with wonder as my wings.

In all my life, and I am an old lady now, I have never fallen under the spell of any land like I fell under the spell of Lightfall Hollow when I was a little girl. It is an enchantment that continues to this day. This is true even though I have resided and travelled in some of the world's most magical regions. Yet, I could never love any of those heavens on Earth the way I love the hollow.

Nor have I ever been charmed by a house, or any human-made structure, including my present-day home in the hollow (a quaint and cozy cabin of my own design), as I was charmed by that cabin of my childhood. This is true even though I have lived in big, beautiful, and expensive homes, as well as visited and worked in some of the world's grandest buildings. Yet, none of those architectural wonders completely captivated me like the little ramshackle cabin my father built.

Lucky for me then my father shared his hunting ground with my mother and me and, along with the hollow, his man cave as our family cottage. Little did Daddy know that what he had really surrendered was the perfect place for his little girl to catch the eye, heart, and hope of a fairy. Or maybe he did.

Chapter Two

LUNA SHADOW

IT HAPPENED on a beautiful autumn night. A full hunter's moon lit up the dark crystal sky above Lightfall Hollow. While the air beneath was crisp and rich with the scent of leaves returning to earth. A ghostly wind blew through, whistling a haunting tune.

My father was working the night shift at the steel mill where he was a laborer in our hometown. It was just my mother and me at the cabin, and my mother, being my mother, would not let me sleep in my favorite top bunk like I wanted. Instead, she insisted I sleep with her in a lower bunk.

I was eight years old. So I knew my mother was being totally irrational and ridiculously overprotective. But no matter how hardily I put up a fight for my due rights and deserved freedom, she refused to be reasoned with, and I ended up in the lower bunk of her choice, silently vowing to stay awake all night in a toss and turn protest. A few moments later, however, I fell peacefully asleep, curled up against my mother, like a snug boat in a safe harbor.

Sometime later, I awakened. A light was shining through the cabin's curtainless bedroom window beneath yucky old George and hitting me square in the face. At first, I thought it was the moon, but this light was more golden in color, and it glowed more warmly, like a candle's flame, and besides, moonlight does not eerily tap against a window as this light had begun to do.

The tapping was as faint as could be, barely audible, yet it was frightening. I could imagine the crumbly, dirt-shrouded skeleton of an indigenous person long dead on the other side of the window, puking yellow flames of poisonous gas from the grave and striking the fragile glass between us with the gnarled bones of a long, accusing finger, angrily pointing at me as an intruder on land not legitimately mine. I put my hands over my ears, squeezed my eyes shut, pulled the bedclothes over my head, and nestled closer to my mother.

Eventually though, my curiosity got the best of me. I uncovered my ears, opened my eyes, and peeked out from beneath the covers. The light was still at it, shining and tapping away. I glanced up at George who, I swear, gave me a wink. I know the head of a dead moose winking a glass eyeball at me should have frightened me even more. But somehow it didn't. Somehow, I found it encouraging. I guess because I had long-known from my father that George was a magical creature and an ally under the strictest of orders by my father to always protect and defend me.

Slowly and stealthily, I pulled away from my mother. My mother was a sound sleeper. Yet, she was also a mother with a mother's finely-tuned radar for detecting and tracking her child's movements. It would not be easy for me to slip out of bed without her noticing my escape.

Then too, I felt a pang of guilt. Earlier in the day, a short time before my mother and I were going to leave our house for the hollow, while my parents assumed I was upstairs, getting ready to go and out of earshot, I had started down the steps that led to our kitchen when I heard my parents talking. I immediately sensed they were talking about me. So, naturally, I sat down on the steps and eavesdropped on their conversation. It seemed my mother was worried about me.

"I'm worried about Lily," I heard my mother say. "She isn't normal, Pete. I'm certain of it. Our daughter is not normal."

"Nonsense, Nora," admonished my father. "Why would you say such a ridiculous thing?"

"I say it because it's true. Lily is peculiar."

"How so?" asked my father.

"Her head is always in the clouds," was my mother's reply. "And so much of the time she's off in another world where no one can reach her. And I mean no one, Pete, not even me, her own mother, can reach her when she's in that other world. It's not normal."

"What other world?"

"A strange other world. A world made up of improbable imaginings and the impractical stuff of fairytales. A dreamer's world. And let me tell you, Pete, it's that land of yours, it's that Lightfall Hollow that is at the bottom of our daughter's starry-eyed delusions. I wish your grandmother had never left you that property, and I wish even more you had never built that cabin."

My father quietly chuckled. "But Lily loves it there. She loves the hollow."

"No! She's obsessed with it! It's the only place she ever wants to be anymore. She begs and begs to go, and then when we're there, she spends hours and hours all alone in the woods, doing heaven only knows what."

"So, she's a nature enthusiast. What's the problem?"

"Pete, I've seen her talking to trees. And then she stands there, nodding her head and making little affirmative noises like the trees are talking back. And, hey, if that's not weird enough for you, it gets even weirder. I have even seen her talking and listening to rocks. Rocks, Pete, rocks!"

"Well, I think that's sweet," my father argued. "Lily is a sensitive child. She knows even rocks have feelings and treasure love and understanding."

"This is not a joking matter, Pete. It's serious, and you should treat it as such. And while we're at it, I think you should stop telling her your silly stories. They only egg her on with her own foolishness."

"Silly stories?" I could hear a distant thunderclap of anger in my father's voice. I wrapped my arms around my folded knees and held on tight.

"Well, all right. Maybe I used the wrong word. I apologize," my mother conceded. "Your stories aren't silly. But you must admit, they're exceedingly outlandish."

"I prefer extraordinarily whimsical."

"Okay. Fine. Your stories are extraordinarily whimsical. Especially the ones about that old moose at the cabin you insist on sending Lily to bed with whenever we're there. That old moose. What's his name again?"

"George. His name is George. And Lily loves my stories. Especially the ones about George."

"Right. George. Now look, Honey, I love your stories too. Even the ones about old George. They're very creative. But the problem is, I think Lily may actually believe them and that has me worried as to where they could lead her or, more accurately, where they could leave her behind. I worry she'll never grow up and live in the real world with the rest of us."

I sighed with relief. I could hear my mother's voice softening. She was beginning to back down a bit. I supposed because she never could bear upsetting my father.

"And I'm telling you there is nothing to be worried about," continued my father. "Lily is just like me as a child, and I grew up okay, didn't I?"

"Pete, you have never grown up. Not really. It is the most infuriating thing about you. Although I must admit it is also the most endearing thing. It makes me crazy, and it makes me crazy for you. So I guess I'm just altogether crazy," said my mother, her voice breaking and becoming squeaky. I recognized that sound. It meant my mother was at the end of her rope and on the verge of tears. Luckily, Daddy also recognized it, and, just like my mother, he never could bear to upset his true love.

"You're not crazy, Nora," said my father, his voice like a warm, gentle rain. "You're wonderful, and I love you."

What followed then were some indistinct murmurings and mushy, kissing sounds that made me feel happy and a little queasy too. I scooted back upstairs to my bedroom and stayed there until my mother knocked on the door and said it was time for us to leave for the hollow.

So, there I was, just a few hours later, thinking of stealing away from my innocently slumbering mother to slyly sneak about in the night in search of something. And that something was most likely a part of the fantastical world that had my mother so worried. Of course, I felt a pang of guilt. However, that didn't stop me. Mostly because I could feel something greater than me, greater even than my mother, beckoning me to come outside, to come outside in the moonlight and wind.

Quiet as a mouse, I scooched out of bed and slid my bare feet into my fuzzy white bunny slippers. The air was chilly, and I knew the air beyond the cabin walls would be a whole lot chillier. I spotted my father's woolen hunting jacket hanging on a wooden peg beside George. I snatched it and put it on over my flannel nightgown. It was way too big, and its bold red and black checks clashed badly with my nightie's delicate pink rosebuds. But I didn't care what I looked like. I was about to embark on an important mission.

I tiptoed to the cabin's front door and silently swung it open. The piercing October air poured in, veiled in a wraithy mist. I froze in my tracks and stood there on my suddenly cold feet, shivering uncontrollably. Perhaps, I thought, this was a bad idea. But then the mysterious, beckoning light was there, right in front of me on the other side of the open door, and there was no turning back. I stepped outdoors, carefully closed the door behind me, and followed the light into the woods. That was when I got my first good look at my very first fairy.

Now at this point in my story, I would not be surprised if you are expecting me to tell you I am a victim of fairy kidnapping. That I was stolen by the fairy, Luna Shadow, to be raised by her tribe. While a fairy child, rejected by fairy society, was left behind in my place for my poor, unsuspecting parents to deal with. But such stories involving swaps of "changelings" for human children are total nonsense.

To begin with, there are no fairy children. Which obviously makes switching fairy children for human children impossible.

Fairies do have offspring, but all fairy children come to their parents and into the world as young adults. We will get to the story behind that in just a bit. But prepare yourself. It will break your heart.

Besides, fairies would never steal the young of any species. Nor would they ever abandon one of their own. There are real reasons, learned through hard experience, for these two critical provisions in the fairy code of conduct, but we will get to that story later too.

Anyhow, going back to that windy, moonlit autumn forest when I was eight years old and met my first fairy, I must admit I did not immediately recognize Luna Shadow as a fairy. This was because I still had the false notion that fairies are stunningly gorgeous beings, like the ones pictured in my books, as well as those portrayed in the kids' movies and TV shows I had seen. But this creature was not in the least bit stunningly gorgeous. She was odd-looking.

Which, as I now know, is normal for a fairy. Although their light, which shines from within and can be turned on and off at will, is pretty, and their wings, since they have had them (which has not been forever), are generally lovely, and though they certainly do not all look alike, a typical fairy is always odd-looking. And Luna Shadow is a typical fairy.

Her skin is as bright white as a late winter moon. While her wings are a dusky gray, the color of shadow cast upon fallen snow. Her body is scrawny, but strong, particularly her hands and feet. Her face has high cheekbones that jut out, a mouth so wide and upturned it stretches from cheekbone to cheekbone, a nose shaped like a lumpy carrot, glittery eyes, pointy ears, and routinely wears the wildest expressions you can imagine. Even though Luna and I have been dear friends for what now seems like forever, there are still times when her strange, otherworldly looks take me by surprise and unnerve me.

As they certainly did the night we met. Luna still teases me about being "scared witless" and "shaking like a leaf" so hard I fell down in the dirt. Put off by my initial, horrified reaction to her, she almost turned and flew away. But, as luck would have it, instead she smiled and said, "Hi."

"Hi," I replied in a tiny, quivery voice as I righted myself into a sitting position. The ground beneath my bottom was freezing, but it also felt solid and reassuring, and, anyway, I knew there was no way my violently quaking legs could support me enough to stand. I remained seated, staring at Luna with what must have been a look of total shock.

"I'm Luna Shadow," Luna announced. "And, in case you're wondering, which you probably are, judging by that 'you could knock me over with a feather' . . . ahem . . . again . . . look on your face, I'm a fairy. To be precise, I'm a proud, full-fledged native member of the oldest fairy tribe in the entire universe, namely the Stone Harvesters of Lightfall Hollow. Like my esteemed predecessors, peers, and progeny, and with the full authorization of our venerable elders, Mother Nature, Father Time, and Papa Space, I am a skilled manufacturer of fairy dust and valiant champion of the honest truth. So, to make a long story short, kiddo, that's who I am. I'm Luna Shadow."

"So now that I've introduced myself to you, all sweetly chummy and proper-like, how about you stop acting like you've encountered a monster, which, by the way, I find very rude and cruelly demeaning, and return the courtesy. You can get the ball rolling by simply telling me your name. Surely you can manage to do that now, can't you?"

Try as I might, I could not get my name out of my mouth. I just kept making these funny little bleating sounds, like I was a helpless baby lamb, crying for her mother.

"Never mind," Luna said after what felt like an eternity of my baby lamb imitation. "I know exactly who you are. You're Dusty Wonders."

Well, that bombshell of a revelation shook me up pretty good. So much so it jolted my voice back into my mouth and put some grit back into my bones.

"I am not," I argued, not forcibly, but at least audibly. "And you're no fairy either."

"But of course, I am. And of course, you are. I'd know you anywhere, Dusty Wonders."

"No," I replied, getting bolder. "I'm telling you, my name is not Dusty, uh, whatever you said. My name is . . ."

"Oh, yeah, I know," interrupted Luna. "But that's just the name your parents gave you. You also have a fairy-given name. And that name is Dusty Wonders. If you don't believe me, you can read it for yourself," said Luna as she opened the enormously thick book she held in her hands and extended it towards me. "Your fairy-given name is listed right here in our *Who's Who of the Magical World*. See. It says right here on this very page, Dusty Wonders, a human female, also known as Lily Moira Bell, daughter of . . ."

"Get that thing away from me," I demanded as I cut Luna short and practically swatted the book out of her hands. "That book is a fake, and so are you. You don't know me, and I sure as heck don't believe you're a fairy. You can't fool me with your lies. I'm not stupid like you think I am."

"Oh, my dear, Dusty Wonders, I would never lie to you. The truth is, I do know you. I know you well. I've known you since your first visit to Lightfall Hollow, riding all googly-eyed and mouth agape on your daddy's shoulders. Since then, I have spent a great deal of my time and energy spying on you, getting to know you better than you know yourself, and I can honestly say I have never once thought of you as stupid. You're human, after all. And on this most beautiful night of all nights, I decided it was high time we meet."

"Why?" I asked in a peevish tone as I crossed my arms over my chest.

"Because, having spent the past five years studying you," answered Luna, "I have become convinced you are your father's daughter."

"What does that mean?"

"What it means is, I believe you are open to the possibility and, therefore, also the knowing of certain things."

"What things?"

"Well, in your particular case, things about me and mine, things about fairies and other magical creatures, our ways, happenings, and experiences here in the hollow and beyond. In other words, our stories."

"You want me to know your stories?" I could feel my jaw dropping and my eyebrows raising in surprise and disbelief. "But I thought fairies were supposed to be super-secret. Like how you make yourselves invisible with magic spells and how you live in trees and even underground. All just so you can always stay hidden away from people."

"Poppycock!" was Luna's sharp retort. "We are always fighting to be seen! It's not our fault humans are so big and full of themselves they hardly ever perceive the magical world right in front of their snubby noses."

"Nonetheless, we are here, Dusty Wonders, and we are sick and tired of trying to get people to notice and pay attention. And that's where you come in. As one of their own, you might have a better chance of getting us what we want."

"But why do you even care?" I inquired, now becoming more interested than irritated.

"We care because, while humans commonly reside in one reality, and we reside in another, Planet Earth is primary home to us both. What happens in the human world is of giant consequence to the magical world. We're a part of one another. We're connected, and we fairies have been doing more than our fair share to maintain that essential connection for quite some time now. But it has become painfully obvious our efforts alone are not enough. We need help. And, again, that's where you come in."

"Then too, as much as we want and need your help, we of the magical world also wish to help you," added Luna. "We feel protective of your species. Compared to us, you are so young and inexperienced. Honestly, you're babies. Yet, you are babies who remind us very much of our younger, infantile selves and thus whom we care about dearly and whose civilization we want to progress as grandly as ours."

"For these reasons, it makes perfect sense to us to pass along to the human world stories of our past, hopefully to inform your messy present. And believe you me, Dusty Wonders, I do not exaggerate when I use the word 'messy.' In fact, I am being generous. You people are a chaotic and disorderly lot. It is downright scary to live on the same globe with such a romper room of crazy kids."

"Yet, we love you," concluded Luna. "We love you as if you were our own children. We are determined to do what we can to evolve humankind and protect what is the most awesome of homes. Third rock from the sun, our fragile and glorious Planet Earth. And, once and for all, that's where you come in."

"Oh, I really don't know about this," I moaned. "This doesn't sound so good to me."

"Please, no whining. It's terribly annoying. Especially when you are so lucky."

"Lucky? How?"

"A path has been opened for you. You need only dare to take the journey. Will you do that, Dusty Wonders?"

"But it all sounds kinda spooky and maybe even dangerous, and I'm a kid," I protested.

"Precisely. You are a child, and come what may, we're depending on you to always remain a child."

"You talk like you think I'm Peter Pan. But I'm just an ordinary kid, and I'll grow up, and then I'll be just an ordinary old person."

"That is also true," agreed Luna. "Nonetheless, you are enough. So now I would like to take you under my wing."

"What does that mean?"

"It means I'll educate you. I'll teach you about the magical world, as well as help you to discover and live it for yourself. Then, at the appropriate time, when you are ready, you will try to relate what you have learned to your fellow humans. You will tell our fairytales."

"But what if they don't believe me?"

"Well, we'll just have to see about that, won't we? So, what do you say? Will you at least try to do your part?" asked Luna.

"Okay, I guess."

"Good enough."

You might be asking, with all my dire misgivings, why I ended up saying yes to Luna. I suppose it was because I am only human. I fancied that, despite her agreeing to my being ordinary, and despite her comparing me to my father, who I knew was also ordinary, she still considered me as an exceptional person. I thought perhaps she saw that, deep down, I was a fair princess. Or, even better, a brave adventurer. Maybe she even glimpsed a little sprinkling of Peter Pan in me too. Which I concluded was very fairy-like of her.

Despite her lack of stunning gorgeousness, it now seemed easy to believe she was whom she said she was. And, wow, how exciting to think that fairies needed me! Needed me so much that one of them was even going to take me under her wing. Which could only mean I would soon be flying like Peter Pan!

First though, I had an even more monumental feat ahead of me. I had to get back in bed, and I had to do so without waking my mother. I was close to succeeding when I made the mistake of trying to warm my frozen feet on my mother's toasty backside. Immediately, she awakened.

"Your feet are like ice, Lily," said my mother as she turned over and took me in her arms.

"Why, you're cold all over. Your skin is as clammy as can be. And what's that in your hair?" she asked, pulling a couple of fallen leaves out of my braid.

"Lily! You've been outside! What in the world for?"

"No, no, I haven't."

"Don't you dare lie to me, Lily Moira Bell. You tell me the truth, young lady, and you tell it to me now."

I don't know what made me say what I said then. It just popped into my head.

"I was riding George."

"You were riding George?"

"Yes. Um. Well, um, he was feeling restless, Mommy, there being a full moon and all tonight, and I didn't think it was right to let him go wandering off in the woods by himself. I felt it was my solemn duty to go with him. So I went outside and climbed on his back, which is invisible, but it is on the outdoor side of the cabin, and once he got his head pulled out of the indoor side, which was quite a terrible struggle, with his big antlers and all, I said, "Giddy-up, George," and off we went. But we're back now, safe and sound. You don't need to worry, Mommy. I know how to take care of myself in the woods."

Perhaps my mother should have punished me then for telling her such a tall tale. But she didn't. Instead, she laughed.

"You get more like your father every day," she said through her chortling. "It is the best thing about you and what I love the most." Then she hugged and kissed me and was soon back in dreamland, comfortable and serene.

So that was how it went on the night I met my first fairy. Despite Luna and my rocky start, it was the beginning of a beautiful friendship that has lasted all these many years. And, as it turns out, Luna was being completely honest with me. I am an ordinary person. Never once have I flown like Peter Pan. Nonetheless, I am enough.

Which brings me to why I am contacting you. At last, it is time for me to do my part. So here goes. We will start at the beginning.

Chapter Three

The Beginning

THE BEGINNING was hundreds of millions of years ago. Earth was going through a period of massive productive change. Tectonic plates were coming together in big bear hugs, forming new and varied lands and waters. While the lands and waters were brimming with evolution, generating new and varied life.

Mother Nature was delighted with her growing, ever-changing brood, but the more its size and diversity increased, the more challenging it became to hold the family together. The ties of kinship were becoming increasingly lengthy and complicated. Communications began to break down. Relationships began to fall apart. Mother Nature was wearing herself out trying to maintain connection. She needed help.

It was to this dead-tired mom the Allegheny Mountains were delivered. Now the Allegheny Mountains are little old squat and stoop-shouldered grandmas. But back then, when they were young and not yet weathered and mellowed by age, they were raw-boned, savage giantesses, as tall and stormy as today's Himalaya Mountains. Yet, their hearts were maidenly and pure. They had pity for Mother Nature. The next time she passed out in exhaustion and collapsed at their feet, the Alleghenies took action. They reached up through the sky and plucked from the heavens tiny pieces of light. They gathered fragments of sunlight, moonlight, and starlight, as well as the light of comets, thunderbolts, rainbows, and any other light they could grab with their bare, big-knuckled hands.

The mountains then flung their harvest down to where Mother Nature slept, pelting her with light. As she awoke from a sweet dream and looked up with a mother's love in her eyes, the sparks transformed, and the first fairies were born. Like all fairies of all ages and places, the most ancient of fairies would become as they still are today, Mother Nature's closest allies and most able assistants.

The Alleghenies had accomplished their mission. To mark their success, the hollow imprint made in the ground by a dreaming Mother Nature became the permanent shape of the land. And in honor of the first fairies and their radiant beginnings, the little valley was given the name it still bears today: Lightfall Hollow.

Yet, the juvenile mountains, however well-intentioned, had acted, not with wisdom, but with the rashness of youth. So the end result was not just sweetness and light. Because, although the fairies were given being, and Mother Nature was given aid, shortly thereafter, a darkness fell upon the world.

What happened is this. When the light was removed from the heavens, the dark it had been brightening was abandoned and left to its own devices. All alone and lost, it changed into something it never should have been, something full of fear, anger, and lies, and it stormed to a place it never should have gone. It invaded Earth.

Mother Nature tried to stop the darkness and send it back to where it came from, but it was a losing battle. A force had been created as strong as she. It was either a fight to the death and the end of all living, or compromise and survival. Even though it meant life from that day forward would wear a shadow, Mother Nature took a leap in the dark, trusting a happy ending was still within reach.

In self-sacrifice, Mother Nature took in as much of the darkness as she could swallow. When that was not enough, and although it broke her heart, she instructed her infant fairies to do the same. This explains why Mother Nature has a persistent cruel streak, as well as why fairies are frequently little dickens.

Still, even after the best efforts of nature and her crew, there was leftover darkness. It ripped into the lands and the waters, attacking and tearing apart everything it found there. It became a part of evolution and life on Earth. This explains why humans are not perfect, as well as why we can even be monstrous.

Nonetheless, the light also persists. This explains why, among all of Mother Nature's kids, including both fairies and humans, there will never be a total monster.

When the first fairies lost their innocence all those millions of years ago, they were cheated out of a childhood, a hardship that has also burdened all following generations. Yet, the fairies refuse to give up on getting back what was stolen from them. This is why they choose to remain so little, as well as why they are so especially fond of children. They're hanging tough in hopes of a more tender age.

Meanwhile, the first fairies wait here in Lightfall Hollow and continue as Mother Nature's helpmates, working to ensure all things that are in existence, have ever been in existence, and will ever be in existence stay connected. "We're all in this whole, great big, wonderful thing together forever." That's the service motto of the first fairies.

Which brings us to the specifics of what the first fairies do for a living and why they are known as the Stone Harvesters of Lightfall Hollow, along with inside information concerning the magical ingredients in fairy dust, its manufacture and use.

Chapter Four

FAIRY DUST

ALL THINGS in the natural world have being. Even a puff of air or a fire's flame has being. And being is about having experiences. Even a fleeting snowflake or a standing boulder has stuff happen to it and stuff it makes happen. It has a story.

But for no lone thing is being a permanent state. All individual things eventually disappear. Nonetheless, when a being exits the physical realm, it leaves behind a memorial of sorts, a magic stone composed of its special and unique story. In fairyland, these most precious of gems are known as remembering rocks.

Each full moon, the first fairies, also known as the Stone Harvesters, travel to all places on Earth and beyond, collecting the latest batch of remembering rocks. They bring the harvested stones back here to Lightfall Hollow where they are milled into fairy dust. Then, at the new moon, other fairies from around the universe fly into the hollow. They cover their wings with a thick coating of the powder and flutter off back to their homes, dusting all things in their wake. If you have ever looked up at the night sky and seen the Milky Way, the hazy band of light you are looking at is not just composed of our galaxy's stars, there are shimmering clouds of falling fairy dust up there too.

It takes a while, but the sprinkled dust eventually settles and seeps into everything everywhere. If you have ever had a night dream, or a daydream, and it seemed like it was not all yours, but belonged as much to someone else, well, that's because motes of fairy dust found their way into your mind. Or if you have ever been somewhere you had never been before, and it looked familiar, that's because specks of fairy dust got into your eyes. Or if you have ever heard a piece of music you had never heard before, and it filled you with longing, but you could not figure out exactly what for, that's because flecks of fairy dust landed in your ears. Or if you have ever met a person you had never met before and felt they were no stranger, but an old friend, that's because particles of fairy dust alighted in your heart.

Fairy dust serves as a gentle reminder that all things are connected, as well as a stern notice to do good work and to do it with all your might. For the universe is like a home built of stones. Too many misplaced, loose, weak, and broken rocks, and the entire house crumbles to ruins.

The Stone Harvesters hope to continue their good work and

make fairy dust here in Lightfall Hollow for a long, long time yet. And I, Dusty Wonders, will add on their behalf they are exceptionally hard and able workers. I often have the privilege of seeing them on the job, and the fairies exert themselves with such skill and energy they literally become balls of fire. It is an electrifying display, as thrilling as any fireworks show.

During their labors, the Stone Harvesters also put on another dramatic performance. For as they grind at their mill, they also sing their motto, "We're all in this whole, great big, wonderful thing together forever." They sing, and they sing until the hollow and surrounding mountains ring with their song. From atop the Alleghenies, the wind picks up the fairy anthem and carries it on, goodness only knows how far.

Next time you find yourself outdoors – or even at a window – and, by the way, you can be in the middle of a big city and still do this, no problem – look for something that is Mother Nature's own. Don't worry. You will recognize it when you see it, and even if it seems small and unimportant, it is not. It counts.

Now, be still, and pay attention. Feel a spirit like your own. Connect and know you are never alone.

When that happens, you can thank the Stone Harvesters. You might even want to leave them some token of your gratitude. Although please don't make your gift anything too extravagant or expensive. As much as fairies delight in presents, they despise excess, and you would not want to end up insulting them. So don't overdo it. Make your gesture of appreciation a thoughtful one that comes from your heart, and the fairies will cherish any little thing you give them.

Having now lectured you about fairy insight for keeping things reasonable, and despite the fact this is going to get me into trouble, I will confide in you that, as advanced as they are, today's fairies, just like we juvenile humans, are a jumble of opposites. (Apparently, evolution is life's longest road.) The best example of this I can give you is how grandiose the first fairies can be when it comes to their names. I refer to this outrageous foolishness as fairy color mania.

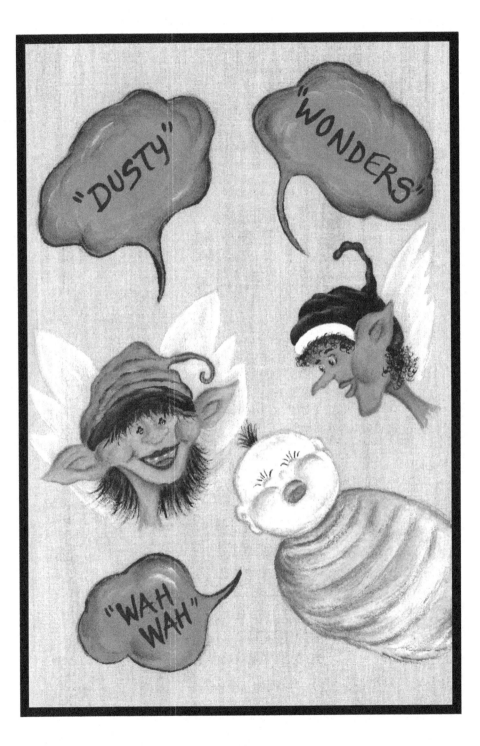

Chapter Five

Fairy Color Mania
(Along with my magic name and yours)

*E*VERY FAIRY everywhere chooses their own name. It is a rite of passage that marks the entrance of a new fairy into the enchanted realm of life. But only the Stone Harvesters take their names from colors and only from colors. It is a long-standing tradition going back to their beginnings. Since light is the source of color, as well as the first fairies.

Although, if you ask me, the custom has gotten way out-of-hand. Oh, it was probably all well and good back when the first fairies were a little clan, and there were enough plain old regular colors to go around. But now there are tons of Stone Harvesters, and it is a point of pride with each one to have a name exclusive to themselves. Fairies can be terribly proud. I wish I had a granted wish for every time I have been sent to a hardware or home improvement store to pick up paint chips for some highfalutin, fancy-pants fairy.

Most often these days, they choose their names from those paint labels too. Misty Lake, Amber Gold, and Forest Hill I can appreciate. I will even go so far as to say I find Granny Smith Apple, Holly Berry, and Jack O Lantern kind of acceptable. But then there are the likes of Cheese Whiz, Stink Bug, Bubble Gum, and -- I kid you not -- my two favorites, Baby Poop and Frog Farts. What were they thinking?

And while we are talking about names, it is not just me, Dusty Wonders, who has a fairy-given name and is listed in the *Who's Who of the Magical World*. The same honors have been given you. Your fairy-given name was awarded within moments of your birth. A fairy whispered it in your ear as a second fairy waited for it to come fluttering out of your other ear. When that happened, the second fairy softly breathed it back to the first fairy. Back and forth and quite a few times over, your fairy-given name was floated through your head like that until at last your brain caught hold and hid the name deep inside its maze for safekeeping. Whereupon you finally quit your bawling like a baby and made first acquaintance with this fascinating world.

But you do not remember that now, do you? Well, not to worry. That is normal. Even if you never get to read about yourself in the fairies' Who's Who, I can assure you, you're there. You matter. You matter a great deal.

In addition, and just as absolutely for sure, your fairy-given name is still inside you, right where your brain tucked it away, and when the time is right, you will not only find it, you will solve it like the secret code it is. Then, wow!

Well, anyhow, speaking of looney behavior, as well as trying to figure things out has reminded me to tell you about the first fairy who started it all. Her name was Red.

Chapter Six

Red

A COMMON FALSEHOOD about fairies is they have a queen. They do not. Although it is true they did have a queen once, a long, long time ago, back when the fairies of Lightfall Hollow were brand-new to life, before they became the Stone Harvesters. Which brings us to Red.

Red was the original fairy. The very first fairy ever. She named herself after the color of the sunrise from which she was made.

Red thought it must be extremely important to be the first fairy. To her mind, it made her superior to the rest of her kind, and for this reason, Red proclaimed herself queen. The other fairies did not protest. They figured Red had a point. Then too, since the fairies were newborns and therefore lacking in world experience, they had no alternative proposals for fairy governance.

So Red became queen. She wasn't a bad queen. Certainly, her intentions were good. She tried to rule fairly and kindly, and she truly did love her subjects.

Still, Red did have a problem. She was bewitched by shiny stuff. She was completely bonkers for it, and she hoarded it in ridiculous amounts. Her castle was crammed so full of gargantuan heaps of cold, hard shiny stuff that Red suffered a constant chill. Since she did not have a single cozy spot to sit or lie down, she was also always tired and cranky. Just as bad, every day Red received more and more cuts, bruises, and lumps on the head from the hourly avalanches of shiny stuff within her bulging palace walls. Worst of all, Red was unhappy, and she did not know how to get rid of her unhappiness.

Red tried to trash her unhappiness by adding to her piles of shiny stuff with new piles of shiny stuff, but it never worked. Well, it would for a little while, but then the unhappiness would return, heavier than ever. Carrying around all that unhappiness made Red mad, really mad, and sometimes she would lose control and be unfair and ugly with her subjects. Afterwards, Red would feel awful about herself and become even more unhappy.

Around and around poor Red went, caught in a cruel circle of an evil spell. It was one she herself had cast and one she, and only she, had the power to break. Although to break such a terrible spell does take terrific effort.

Despite Red's bouts of bad temper, the other fairies adored her, but they adored her only because she was queen, simply assuming that being queen and having the most shiny stuff made

Red the greatest fairy of them all. The sad fact of the matter was that none of the other fairies knew Red in the way she needed to be known. No one knew her in her heart of hearts. Although that did not stop the other fairies from trying to be like the Red they put on a pedestal and prized from a distance.

For example, the fairies took the power structure Red had begun when she declared herself queen and added to it. They made a hierarchy that ranked each fairy according to their importance to fairy society. The result of this hierarchy was the fairies were divided and arranged in separate groups at different levels. No longer were they all together as a team, with each one as free, special, and treasured as every other one.

Some of the divisions were high up, closest to the top and Queen Red. There were not many of these divisions and not too many fairies were in them. Other divisions were in the middle. These divisions had more fairies than the upper divisions. While the remaining divisions were on the bottom. These divisions had by far the most members. If you have ever seen people in a human pyramid, you get the picture. (If not, you can probably find a photo of one.) Except the fairies did not make their pyramid with fairy bodies, they made it with fairy lives.

You probably would like to know what they used to determine a fairy's worth. Once again, they followed Queen Red's lead and used shiny stuff as their measurement tool. Those fairies who had the most shiny stuff were placed in the highest division. These individuals were considered the cream of fairy society, and they received more respect, rights, privileges, and opportunities, as well as the freedom to pick from a hugely wider variety of choices than those fairies in the lower levels. And so it went.

The fairies had not yet learned there is a great deal of luck involved when it comes to getting shiny stuff. Being in the right place at the right time is a lot of it. But, like I said before, back then, the fairies were no more than babes in the woods. All they knew was they wanted to be like their queen, and their queen evidently believed shiny stuff to be the best thing ever.

Idolizing their queen, the fairies got caught in the same evil spell as she. Everything became about getting more and more shiny stuff. They worked their fool heads off, and they broke their poor hearts as they came to see one another as rivals, distrusting and fussing with each other as everybody tried to pass by everybody else and clamber atop the heap as the lone one.

Now, just like Queen Red, everyone else was unhappy. Also, just like Queen Red, they did not know how to get rid of their unhappiness, and their unhappiness made them unfair and unkind. Even worse, behaving unfairly and unkindly became more and more accepted in fairy society until eventually the fairies were not even aware of their unfairness and unkindness.

It is not surprising then that the fairies in the higher divisions of the fairy hierarchy began to use the fairies in the lower divisions to do their work, something the fairies of the lower divisions did not have the freedom to say no to since the choices and possibilities open to them were so few. To survive, they had to take the jobs permitted them. Even fairies have to eat.

As you might suspect, the most grueling and dangerous work was assigned to the fairies of the lower divisions. For example, since practically all the shiny stuff on land had already been collected and hoarded, the lower division fairies were forced to dig for gemstones and crystals, slaving in the dirt and dark of a deep mine that sometimes collapsed down upon them. Or they were forced to dive for pearls and seashells, slaving in the salt and dark of a deep ocean that sometimes crashed down upon them. Or they were forced to steal baby bird eggs and dragonfly wings, slaving in the dank and dark of a deep shame that sometimes crushed down upon them.

Just as humiliating for the lower division fairies was how ignored and forgotten they were. It was like they were not even fairies anymore, but some other lesser, disgusting creatures or, worse, did not exist at all. Under such circumstances, it is a wonder the lower divisions were able to hang on to their self-worth. While it is no wonder, desperate for any recognition whatsoever, even if it were negative, a few of them turned to stealing shiny stuff. Or sometimes they would even destroy shiny stuff.

As I have indicated, almost all the shiny stuff in Red's queendom was owned by herself and the small number of fairies in the upper divisions. About 99% of the whole shiny stuff pie was theirs. Which I think you will agree should have been more than enough, with plenty of pie to spare. But because the fairies in the upper divisions measured their importance, value, power, and even their goodness with shiny stuff, losing even a teeny-tiny bit of it, or even suspecting they might lose a teeny-tiny bit of it, made them frightened.

The upper division fairies were further frightened because, in thoughts hidden even from themselves, they knew they were wrong to be unfair and unkind to their fellow fairies. And while dreadful thoughts like that can be imprisoned in the dark, there is no stopping them from trying to break out into the light. Such workings of the mind are like ghouls locked in an attic. Although out of sight, their constant bumping about in the night is terrifying. So here is an interesting question for you. What do you think would happen if such ghouls were set free?

The upper divisions were full of fear, and their fear made them angry. They then took their fear and anger out on the lower divisions, making the lives of the fortuneless even more left behind, neglected, poor, and enslaved. While they themselves stayed chained in a torture chamber of fear and anger.

For everyone involved, it was no way to live, and the fairies became more and more unhappy. While Queen Red was the unhappiest of all. Because she truly did love her subjects, and their unhappiness weighed upon her even more than her own. Yet, by herself, she could not seem to figure out what to do. She needed help.

Queen Red went to visit the elders. She went to see Mother Nature, Father Time, and Papa Space to ask for their advice. However, although the oldsters closely listened, they answered her sad worries with nothing other than silence. I am certain they had their reasons, but it was very upsetting for Queen Red when the only parents she had ever known offered her no words of wisdom. It made her feel as if she were all alone in the world. Downhearted and forlorn, she returned to her castle, where her giant piles of shiny stuff no longer appeared quite so dazzling and life itself was dull.

Thank goodness then, not long afterwards, something wonderful happened. A lower-division fairy called Blue, who had named himself after the color of an open, limitless sky and who was on the crew of those assigned to steal baby bird eggs and dragonfly wings, refused to do such mean and meaningless labor. Encouraged by his honorable action, other fairies who were charged with the same miserable task united with Blue and also refused to steal baby bird eggs and dragonfly wings. They caused such a stir the other lower-division drudges were moved to join them, and soon no more shiny stuff was being harvested.

The upper divisions were more than a little miffed. They thought the lower divisions were being just awful and bad. So they decided to issue a complaint with Queen Red.

Queen Red was in her garden, escaping her castle's gloom. Although it was a friendly, lovely garden, it was her first visit there. She was surprised how good it felt to breathe fresh air, curl up among the flowers, and lie in the sun, listening to the birds sing and watching dragonflies flit here and there. She felt almost happy, and she fell into a comfortable sleep.

She could have slept like that forever. However, the perturbed fairies of the upper divisions awakened her, making their case against the lower divisions in loud, angry voices. Curious about what she was being told, Queen Red peered over her garden wall at the poorer quarters of the fairy village where the lower divisions had their homes.

What she saw there amazed her. The lower division fairies had come together to care for one another. They were treating every individual with consideration, respect, and dignity, as though each was the most important fairy of all. They were sharing their food and whatever else anyone needed. They were even happily sharing their tiny little, meager amounts of shiny stuff. In sum, they were being kind and fair.

Then the truth struck Queen Red, and she knew why she was unhappy. In addition, she knew what she needed to do. She knew these things because Queen Red truly did love her subjects.

To begin with, although it was not easy for her, she got rid of her excess shiny stuff. Now, mind you, she did not get rid of all of it. Because there is nothing basically wrong with having shiny stuff. In fact, shiny stuff is good for helping make life enjoyable, precious memories, and the world a more beautiful place.

Nonetheless, Queen Red ended up giving away most of her shiny stuff to her subjects. Although by the time she was done with the redistribution, they were no longer her subjects. Because she had also given up her queendom. Now she was just Red, living in the fairy village with her friends. And especially Blue.

From the moment their eyes met, Red and Blue were spun about in a whirlwind romance. They married, and together they had a son who would choose as his name Purple Mountain Majesty, a name which met with some disapproval within the fairy community for being too snooty. But Purple Mountain Majesty, despite his full name being a fancy mouthful, was not the high and mighty type. In fact, it was he who wrote the Stone Harvesters' hit song, "We're all in this whole, great big, wonderful thing together forever." The words and melody came straight from his heart, and he lived his entire life according to its message.

It is also true Purple Mountain Majesty was his own fairy. Which is why he typically went by his middle name, Mountain. That choice did not sit well with all the fairies either. But that was Mountain for you. He was always looking forward. Although he understood traditions are valuable things, he also realized established practices are not the be all and end all. They have their limitations.

At this point in this story, you may be expecting me to tell you Red and the rest of the fairies lived happily ever after. But real life is not like that. True happiness always has spots of sadness, like bruises on a peach.

Although Red got over her addiction to shiny stuff, many of the other fairies remained under its spell, and there was nothing Red could do about that other than sympathize and be generous with her compassion. It took eons of struggle and lots of unhappiness before all the fairies learned the lesson Red had learned, and they lived undivided again in freedom, cooperation, understanding, and love, as they still do today.

As for Red, off and on during her years on Earth, she faced other challenges and lived through other sad and hard times. But she also realized a resilient joy that lifted her up when life threw her down, and she never felt again like she was all alone in the world.

When she died, and, oh, that brings up another common misconception about fairies, that they are immortal and never die. By their own choice, fairies are not immortal, and they do die. Although it is true a fairy can live an enormously long time, much, much longer than any human. Yet, all fairies are wise enough to eventually let go of life and die.

When Red died, just like every other being, she left behind a remembering rock. The Stone Harvesters treated it in their usual way, grinding it into fairy dust and sprinkling it throughout the universe to exist forever as one with all things. So Red is in your blood, and do not forget it. Like I told you before, you are never alone.

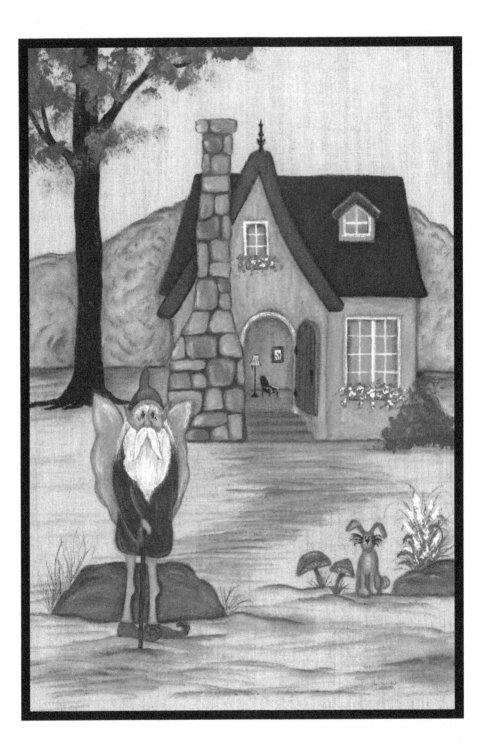

Chapter Seven

GLAMOUR AND THE HOUSE OF GOLD

KNOWING RED'S story, you have learned the truth about two standard notions regarding fairies. One, they have a queen. They do not. Two, they are immortal. They are not.

While we are at it then, I would like to take the opportunity to shed light on some other prevailing views concerning fairies that, while they have some truth to them, do not give the whole picture. The first is about something called glamour.

There are two types of glamour. One is an extremely elegant physical appearance that produces fascination in its observers. Unicorns were excellent examples of beings with this type of glamour. I say "were excellent examples" because today there are no unicorns. They ceased to exist when they gave up their glamour for something more beautiful. But we will get to that story later. At present, I am just trying to get us to the second type of glamour.

The second type of glamour is a fairy spell that hides the existence of the magical world from humans. Under its enchantment, people are presented with a false reality. It was invented for the protection of magical creatures soon after humans began appearing on Earth because, as Luna rightly stated on the night we met, "People are so big and full of themselves."

Glamour is the reason why some say the fairies are shapeshifters, that if a fairy so wishes, they can transform themselves into another being. But that is not true. For example, a fairy cannot change into a dog. However, through the power of glamour and the illusions it creates, a fairy can make you see a dog instead of their true fairy self.

Which sounds cool, and I am sure you can sympathize with the desire to stay safe, but hiding the magical world from humans turned out to be a mistake. It put up a wall between our two realms, a division the fairies have come to realize is harmful to both sides. Now they work to overcome their fears, tear down the wall, and reunite.

The problem is, because we humans are so big and full of ourselves, we are difficult to reach. But not impossible. And you can help. Because you have a superpower that can chip away at the wall that glamour built.

As to what that superpower is, I will remind you of it soon.

First though, I want to continue correcting some common misconceptions about fairies, as well as tell you about Gold and his house.

Since you have never visited the magical world (or at least not since you were extraordinarily young and could see through walls), I suspect you believe what I did until Luna set me straight. You probably believe fairies make their homes inside trees, hills, caves, lakes, and other hidey-holes. While it is true fairies dwell in those places, such living quarters are always temporary.

For example, if a tree is ailing, fairies will move in and care for the tree until it either returns to health or dies. Or, if a hill is feeling lonely, fairies will crash the hill and throw parties 24/7 until the hill has had enough of socializing and appreciates the value of some solitude every now and again. Or, if a cave is down in the mouth, fairies will hang around the cave and do their silliest bat impersonations until the cave's stalagmites and stalactites are flashing in ear-to-ear grins. Or, if a lake is agitated and churning in anger, fairies will settle within its waters and conduct meditation sessions until the lake is calm and still.

But such occupancies are always temporary. Where fairies make their permanent residences is above ground, pretty much the same way humans do. Although not since the time of Queen Red has there been a fairy palace. There are no fairy mansions these days either. This is not to say, however, that fairy dwellings are not lovely. They are lovely, and each one is a unique original. While this is true, it is also true that all fairy abodes are modeled on the home built by Gold.

Gold is the universe's oldest living fairy. Like Red, he was born here in Lightfall Hollow as one of the first fairies. He named himself after the color of the shooting star from which he was made. Which proved to be ironic. Since the shooting star was gone inside of Gold's first heartbeat. While Gold himself goes on and on. In fact, there is a rumor that sometimes floats through the magical world that Gold is immortal. But since Gold is considered the wisest of fairies, the suggestion of him being fool enough to never let go of this world and make way for greater life is always dismissed as the hooey it is.

Back during the reign of Queen Red, Gold was the sole fairy who was never blinded by shiny stuff. He saw Queen Red's glamourous palace as the unwelcoming, uninspired place it was. For his own home, Gold wanted something more friendly and imaginative. But he needed the right inspiration. Which is what he finally received when people began appearing on Earth.

Gold was one of the first fairies to catch sight of us strange newcomers. After some observation, he was concerned. The magical world had run things on Earth for as long as he could remember. Now Gold could envision humans taking over. He worried about losing power. He worried about his way of life disappearing. He worried about getting dumped.

But Gold did not allow his fears to command him. So, of course, he was awed and amazed when he beheld the human children. As you will recall, fairies do not get a childhood. Gold had never been a kid. Nor had he ever had the experience of seeing kids being kids.

As he watched the children play and invent incredible new things with their imaginations, Gold thought he had never seen anything so beautiful, powerful, or wonderful. He realized his world had been missing something magical. He recognized humans as extraordinary additions to Earth's family.

Gold also grasped something more as he watched the children play. He got the inspiration he had been wanting to make his home the whimsical little cottage with its open door that still exists today as the dream home of all fairies. I expect it would be your dream home too. I know for sure you would feel welcome and excited to play there. Unfortunately though, glamour continues to get in the way.

As I said, there were other fairies besides Gold who spotted us newbies. But those fairies were not so impressed. I do not know why. Those fairies are now long gone, so I can't ask them, and if Gold knows, he isn't saying. Perhaps those other fairies never noticed the kids. Or if they did, they did not take a good look. Perhaps their fear of being replaced was so all-consuming, they were trapped in a panic, and when you are trapped in a panic, a lot of your perceptions go wonky.

It was those fairies who conjured up glamour and convinced their peers that hiding the magical world from humans was a smart and practical thing. Gold voted against the scheme, as did a few others, but they were largely outnumbered. The spell was cast, and a wall went up. Earth was no longer the open, free, and undivided place it was always meant to be.

Afterwards, there were those who tried to make life difficult for

Gold. A band of banshees took to hounding him, pursuing Gold with yowls about death coming soon to traitors. But Gold was no traitor, and anyone with any sense could see that, and over time, Gold showed them a lot more too. Now all magical creatures, banshees included, look up to him as their beloved sage.

Incidentally, Gold forgave the banshees. When I asked him why, he said he learned a long time ago that he is not perfect. Since then, forgiveness has been a no-brainer.

I suppose that helps explain why Gold and Boogeyman are so close. I haven't gotten to Boogeyman's story yet. If you can hold on though, I will.

Now for your superpower. It is your imagination. When you use your imagination as an inventive force, you change the world. You give life something new, and there is nothing more beautiful, powerful, and wonderful than that.

Additionally, when you use your imagination as an inventive force, you free your mind, and a free mind can see through any fakery. There's no hiding from a free mind. No wall can block the entrance of a free mind.

These are the wisdoms Gold learned as he watched children play and exercise their imaginations.

So play, and play often. Be a champion of creative play. And, as you share your superpower, know that nearby is Gold, watching and waiting for the wall that divides and confines to come down, hoping someday he can be with you for real in the restored world with its open door you both deserve. It is what he lives for.

Chapter Eight

WINGS

IT WAS sometime after the first fairies finally got their act together and lived again in harmony they came up with the idea of making fairy dust from remembering rocks and dispersing it throughout the universe. No longer held captive by shiny stuff and grateful to be living in freedom, they wanted to give back and contribute something useful. Something to help share the magnificence of every existence, including their own lives. And, of course, your life too.

The fairies put together a rough draft of their plan and ran it by Mother Nature, Father Time, and Papa Space, hoping for their approval. Which they got in a big way. Since the elders were tickled pink with the fairies' plan. Mother Nature was delighted because she was going to get some help keeping the oneness of all things a natural fact. Father Time was pleased because he was going to get some help keeping the existence of each individual thing ever in the present. While Papa Space was happy because he makes room for joy in absolutely everything.

A word about Father Time and Papa Space. Father Time's purpose in life is hard on him. Inside a gnarled and rugged exterior beats a tender heart. Which aches every time he watches a being he has known since the thing's youth grow old and die. Or worse, die before he can grant more of what is his to give. It causes him an agony that would be unbearable if Time did not have as his partner and match, Space, to love and support him. The two are inseparable, and that is lucky for us. Because where would we be without time and space?

Regarding Papa Space, as alike, close, and coequal as he is to his husband, he is more lighthearted. The fairies, being naturally attracted to high spirits, get a real kick out of him. They do a lot of whooping it up together, and many of the merrymaking high jinks, pranks, and larks the fairies are famous for have as their mastermind Papa Space.

But back to the Stone Harvesters' business enterprise. The elders helped the fairies iron out the details and finalize their proposal for a worthy profession. The plan was then adopted with every fairy voting in its favor. Afterwards, it was Papa Space who declared the first fairies "Stone Harvesters," the name by which they still proudly go even as I write this.

In addition to their societal name, it was during this legendary work session the Stone Harvesters received wings. Previously, they had been wingless, and they could not fly. Conditions which the fairies took for granted. But when they were developing their business plan, a major concern was how to carry out the included jobs in a timely fashion. Although, by then, there were other fairy societies populating Earth, along with the rest of the universe, and all had agreed to provide fairy dust delivery service, travel between many communities was hopelessly lengthy. Even with the extra help, it was not going to be possible to set reasonable deadlines for project completions. Especially when the Stone Harvesters were starting with a humongous backlog of remembering rocks to be collected and somehow lugged to Lightfall Hollow.

When confronted with this fairy fret, Mother Nature came to the rescue as she so often does by offering an astonishing, while also obvious and practical solution. She told the Stone Harvesters to get wings. She further advised they should get wings both heavy-duty and capable of flying at warp speed. Although the fairies realized having such wings would change their lives in ways both apparent and yet unknown, after some careful consideration, they decided it was worth taking the chance.

So the Stone Harvesters got wings. Just like that, they got wings sturdy enough to transport heavy loads and miraculously swift. Then they asked all fairies everywhere to get such wings. Which they did. Just like that. Although they all still needed to learn how to fly.

You might think the fairies received their wings the way they did because there was more magic in those long-ago, bygone days. But that is not true. There is more magic now than ever. Because magic, just like everything else on the good Earth, evolves and branches out. Clover and Cricket proved that. The story of those two master magicians is coming up shortly.

Chapter Nine

FLIGHT SCHOOL

S O NOW every fairy everywhere had wings. They were real beauties too. On top of that, Mother Nature surprised the Stone Harvesters by adding a little extra pizzazz to theirs. She made each fairy's wings in the same color as their name. For the most part, they turned out lovely.

Nonetheless, even way back then, a few of the Stone Harvesters had chosen names a tad unconventional. These included the likes of Rat Tooth, Slug Slime, Tooshie Rash, as well as the twins, Pus and Barf Glop. You know, you got to wonder if Mother Nature was not also playing a little prank on those screwballs. If there is one thing I know about Mother Nature, it is that she has a wicked sense of humor.

She may have met her match in the fairies. Because Rat Tooth,

Slug Slime, Tooshie Rash, as well as the twins, Pus and Barf Glop were as delighted with their wings as any other fairy, and they wore them just as proudly. Likewise, as you are aware, even today, while understanding their wings will take on their chosen color, there are still Stone Harvesters who insist on picking the craziest names imaginable. What a bunch of clowns.

Now it was time to learn to fly, and the Stone Harvesters got right to it. However, try as they might, they could not get their wings to work. If you know what it is like when a car's battery is dead, and the car will not start, but just makes a clicking or whining sound, well, that is what it was like with the fairies' wings. They even made those same annoying sounds, as though their wings were tongues clicking in disapproval and whining in complaint.

The Stone Harvesters thought perhaps all that was needed was a little jump start. So they tried to give their wings an energy boost by doing things like bouncing high in the air on a trampoline, jumping from a swing in full swing, leaping from a springboard, running off a cliff, etc., but with no success, oodles of screaming in terror, and some minor-to-moderate injuries. It was frustrating.

Father Time had come by to watch the fairies' antics. Papa Space had told him he needed a laugh, and the fairy flight school was the perfect location to find one. Papa Space was right. Because Father Time practically split his gut laughing at the Stone Harvesters' attempts at flight. Eventually though, he felt sorry for the wannabe flyers and decided to do what he could to help.

As you surely realize, Father Time has seen everything under the sun and then some. Even more extraordinary, he remembers it all. He knew why the wings refused to fly. It was because of a disgraceful chapter in the history of the fairy race.

Although it had happened ages ago, Father Time could remember the bad old days when the Stone Harvesters had thieving hands and greedy hearts. He could recall the horrendous suffering the fairies had caused by robbing birds of their families and dragonflies of their freedom. He could dig into the past and bring to light those ugly realities, giving them the power, despite their ugliness, to make the world a more beautiful place.

While the fairies before him could not. Because they had been kept ignorant. They had never been told the whole truth about themselves. They had never been informed of the bad stuff that, like the good stuff, went into making their lives. Well, actually, they had been told watered-down pieces and sugarcoated slices of fairy evil. But because what they had been fed was as bland and sweet as milk toast, while easy to swallow, it nourished no growth.

Father Time gathered the Stone Harvesters together in a circle and taught them the history lesson they had never had, and without which, they would never fly. To say the least, it was a difficult education, and some might even say the fairies should have been spared the pain it caused them. But Father Time believes the wee folk and the power of their love are not to be underestimated.

Father Time is apparently right too. Because his telling the whole story to the fairies caused them to become sensitive to bird and dragonfly lives. Previously, they had just looked the other way and paid no mind to their fellow creatures. But now the Stone Harvesters began to take heed, and they realized the birds and dragonflies were still not receiving the liberty and justice they deserved, and it was time to do something about that.

The Stone Harvesters asked the birds and dragonflies for a meeting. Thank goodness their invitation was accepted. At the meeting, the fairies basically said four things to the birds and dragonflies. One, they admitted they and their race had been wrong. Two, they apologized from the bottom of their hearts. Three, they promised to forevermore treat birds and dragonflies the same as themselves. Four, they asked what they could do to repair the damage that had been done. Which, of course, they knew was not anywhere near possible, but it was a sincere offer, and the birds and the dragonflies took them up on it and made their requests. Which the fairies acted upon pronto.

Afterwards, the world was a more beautiful place. As for the Stone Harvesters, their wings began to work, and they could fly. Which they did and do. Just like that.

Chapter Ten

Izzy

ONCE THE Stone Harvesters got their wings to work, they were able to help all fairies everywhere take flight as well. Soon the entire fairy species was up and flying around the universe. Now it was time to get down to business.

There was much debate among the Stone Harvesters about which remembering rock should have the honor of being the first ever to be harvested and milled into fairy dust to, sooner or later, become a part of you. Red had recently died, and many thought it would be appropriate to pay her the tribute, but her son, Purple Mountain Majesty, better known as Mountain, opposed the idea. He said it was not what his mother would have wanted. After all, she had given up her queendom to join in solidarity with the common folk, and she had never regretted it.

It would not be proper to, once again, put her upon the pedestal she had chosen to come down from.

As a more suitable candidate, Mountain nominated one of his all-time personal heroes, Izzy. Mountain was certain Izzy would have had no objection to being placed atop a pedestal. He had been on the bottom for so long.

Mountain was a gifted persuasive speaker. He always knew his subject matter inside and out, and he respected his listeners, even those who disagreed with him. He never spoke in a hateful, looking-for-a-fight voice, and he never tried to dominate and control. On the contrary, Mountain reasoned with his audience. He spoke in calm, matter-of-fact tones and used words that were rational, honest, and appropriate to the point he was trying to make.

When the fairy votes were tallied, Izzy had won by a landslide. Mountain's mother would have been proud. While his dad, Blue, stood up and yelled at the top of his lungs, "That's my boy!" Which embarrassed Mountain to no end. But such is a parent's right.

You may be wondering who this Izzy fellow was. Obviously, with a name like Izzy, he was not a Stone Harvester. (There is not a single color I know of that goes by the name of izzy.) Nor was he a fairy at all. Izzy was a little sea creature from way back when. Back before there were Allegheny Mountains, fairies, and Lightfall Hollow. Although he was not born magical, by virtue of his diligent and imaginative efforts, Izzy became magical, and his magic advanced the world.

Chapter Ten

As I have already described it to you, these days Lightfall Hollow is a small, hidden, woodland valley. From her heart, trees soar up like wings. The trees fly through the hollow and up the hillsides, guardian angels in formation. They make a deep, feathery forest out of what was, millions and millions of years ago, the mud bottom of a shallow ocean.

Fossils of the little shelled sea creatures that once lived in the mud of the ocean floor can still be found in the soil. These are the stones that I, Dusty Wonders, like to harvest. I find the fossils fascinating.

So I have something in common with Mountain. Although I never met him. Since he died way before I was born. But I have been told by his great-grandchildren that Mountain collected fossils too, and that is how he came to have as a role model an ancient sea creature. Because fossils are also a kind of remembering rock, and because Mountain understood their language, the fossils recalled to him the adventures of a little shelled sea creature named Izzy.

At the start of Izzy's story, under the Appalachian Sea, all was dull, murky, and mucky. It was life, but it was not much of a life, and Izzy and his fellow little sea creatures galumphed through it with no purpose and no fun. Until one day Izzy bothered to look up and saw a sunbeam piercing through the gloom.

"Look at that! It's awesome!" exclaimed Izzy.

"Hmm. Whatever," replied the other little sea creatures.

"I've never seen anything like it," said Izzy. "It looks friendly and sweet, yet scary and dangerous too."

"Whatever," repeated the others.

"It makes me want to hide," continued Izzy, "but I am also attracted to it. I get the feeling it needs me, and I need it."

"Whatever."

From then on, Izzy paid close attention to the light. Again and again, he tried to reach out to it. However, when you are a little sea creature with a small, mushy body largely cooped up in a tight, hard shell, your ability to reach out is extremely limited. Izzy realized he needed help.

"Hey, gang, how about we all pile up, one on top of the other, with me at the very tip top, and make a huge, gigantic line up out of the ocean and into whatever lies beyond. Let's go check out the mystery," urged Izzy.

"No way," replied the other little sea creatures.

"Come on, guys. Wouldn't you like a little adventure in your lives?" asked Izzy.

"No way," repeated the others.

"Who knows? Maybe we'll make an important discovery. Don't you guys ever want to do something great?"

"No way."

Even after his friends did not see things his way and could not be persuaded to rally to his cause, Izzy continued to focus on the light. So he began to see even more.

Izzy saw there were different kinds of light. He studied the strong blazes of the sun's light and the soft echoes of the moon's light. On crystal clear nights, he considered the twinkles of distant stars. During electrical storms, he pondered the flashes of nearby thunderbolts. He wondered at the bent, colored light of a couple of rainbows, and once there was a meteor shower, and Izzy stared awe-struck at the straight-shooting streaks of fireballs.

All this learning made Izzy all the more curious, and he became determined to reach the unknown. So he got creative.

"Excuse me, sir," said Izzy to the next fish that swam by him. "Excuse me, but do you think I might catch a ride with you?"

"Ah. I guess so," replied the fish.

"Thank you, sir. That is very kind," said Izzy, clamping his shell on to the fish's tail. "Any chance you're swimming up to the end of the ocean?"

"Heavens, no. I'm much too small to make such a big journey," denied the fish. "Besides, who knows what's up there? I've heard tales of monsters."

"Oh, I see," sighed Izzy.

After that first short ride, which, unsurprisingly, ended back on the ocean floor, Izzy decided to get good at jumping from fish to fish. He figured if he could get enough rides with upward swimming fish, he would be able to reach the end of the ocean. However, when you are a little sea creature with a small, mushy body largely cooped up in a tight, hard shell, your ability to get good at jumping from upward swimming fish to upward swimming fish is extremely limited. Every time Izzy tried, he failed.

"What a dreamer you are, Izzy," jeered the other little sea creatures. "Hang it up, you silly fool. Just stay in the mud where you belong. You don't want to end up looking like a loser."

"No," replied Izzy. "I just have to keep trying."

And he did. Over and over again, Izzy tried to reach the light. Each time, he failed.

Meanwhile, the ocean was bored stiff with her own shallow existence, and she had been sleeping it away. "Same old same old," snored the ocean.

So Izzy's gumption was something new to the ocean, and her slumber was disturbed. It did not matter the waves Izzy made were tiny and their source was the failed trying of a small, simple, awkward creature. The ocean was energized.

"What keeps tickling me?" murmured the ocean as she wriggled in her sleep.

Little sea creatures do not live long, and Izzy soon died. He still had not reached the light. Instead, the mud he had tried to rise above covered him. Then more mud buried him even deeper. More mud came after that.

"I am sorry I never reached you," said a dying Izzy to the light. "I wanted so much to help my world become greater. But at least I lived to improve myself," finished Izzy as he brightened up and beamed like the sun.

After his death, Izzy's body quickly washed away and merged with the sea. While his shell was slowly worn away by the minerals in the water that oozed through the mud layers on the ocean floor. The minerals made an empty space, called a mold, in the shape of Izzy's shell.

At the same time this was happening, the mud was becoming more and more thick and heavy. The mud was turning into rock. When the mud finally finished hardening into rock, Izzy's fossil was complete.

You might think we have reached the end of Izzy's story, but that is not true. Because after Izzy died and his fossil was buried, the ocean finally awoke and arose to great heights. She heaved up her floor and crashed it about, lifting the rock layers and forming them into mountains. The dull world of the Appalachian Sea had reached the light at last, and Izzy was the initial force that began the journey.

Izzy had caused the ocean to move. It was no more than a wriggle, but that wriggle led the ocean to give a little shake. Then she shifted and rolled over, and things really got rolling.

"Thank you, Izzy. Thank you," rejoiced the newborn mountains. "We love you, and your spirit will live forever." Then, to make good their promise, as well as to celebrate their bursting forth from darkness into light, the Allegheny Mountains did something extraordinary. They laughed. The first laughter ever. The mountains laughed and laughed.

As you probably know, laughter is contagious. Happening to

be in the neighborhood, Papa Space heard the mountains laughing. He was so charmed by their creation, he tried it out for himself. It was not long before he was shrieking in merriment, pausing only to invite Father Time and Mother Nature to get in on the fun. Things really got jolly then. As other beings from around the universe got wind of this new universal language and joined in. Soon everyone on Earth and beyond was laughing. All in all, it was a good day.

Since that day, laughter has been the favorite form of communication of the magical world. Because, like fairy dust, laughter is a connector. It brings us together. No matter how far apart we may be from one another and no matter how unable we are to touch one another, laughter draws us as close as any hug, kiss, or cuddle.

Although, truth is, sometimes it is impossible to laugh. Terrible things happen, and they hurt so badly they cannot be laughed at or laughed away. Thank goodness then that laughter is excellent at waiting. No matter how long it takes, it will always wait for you. It will always wait for you because laughter has in its bedrock the courage, determination, patience, imagination, and hope of a little magical sea creature named Izzy.

Chapter Eleven

GIANTS, GOOD AND NAUGHTY

S O IT was that Izzy's remembering rock became the first ever to be milled into fairy dust to live within you. As for Izzy's fossil, Mountain returned it to the spot where he had found it. To this day, it is here in Lightfall Hollow, resting in peace in the bed of the feather forest, watched over by the guardian trees. And that is a fine thing indeed.

During the past few thousand years, many different trees of many different varieties have stood in Lightfall Hollow. The Stone Harvesters have loved, and still do love them all like the kindred magical beings they are. Plenty of times, I have watched the fairies hugging and giving butterfly kisses to the trees currently living here. The oaks, hickories, maples, locusts, and their relatives.

I have also seen the fairies mourning for their tree friends now gone. They especially grieve for the trees that did not die a natural or meaningful death, but were taken before their time by careless, ignorant humans. These include the hemlocks and white pines that mainly made up Pennsylvania's forests until the majority of these dignified, solemn, and towering trees were chopped down for their wood. The mass butchery continued for more than one hundred years. When the slaughter finally ended, all that remained of the magnificent giants were dismembered stumps, left to waste upon an empty land. It was sad for all of Pennsylvania, including Lightfall Hollow, where the Stone Harvesters were so bummed out, they considered quitting their jobs and leaving the universe behind.

But Mother Nature gave them a stern talking-to for even considering such a selfish thing, and then life, as life always does, went on. It is just the way it is with Mother Nature. Even when you think she ought to give up and call it a day, she never does, and I have it on good authority she never will.

This does not mean, however, that Mother Nature's patience is without end. She does punish those who routinely, knowingly, and continually offend her. Just look at what she did to the Cyclopes.

If you have never heard that story, the Cyclopes were giants with only one eye. They only had one eye because they were not interested in seeing more. They never cleaned up, so they were filthy, home to swarms of vermin, and they reeked of their own rot.

Much worse than their lack of good hygiene was the Cyclopes thought they were better than everyone else. The only rule they followed was it was every giant for themselves and only for themselves. They consumed every treasure on Earth they could get their hands on, and they ate humans and other creatures alive because they were that unfeeling regarding the pain and suffering of others.

If that were not bad enough, the Cyclopes, who had as their profession the making of objects forged from iron, were irresponsible and destructive businesspeople. Their business doings were so reckless, wasteful, and excessive, they caused natural disasters, like hurricanes, floods, and fires, that were not really natural at all, but the result of the violent pounding of the giants' hammers rattling the world and the raging fires of their furnaces overheating the globe.

The saddest thing is, the Cyclopes were not born that way. As children, they had been quite sensitive, highly tuned in to the world's wonders, and focused with both eyes and whole hearts on the welfare of others. They were some of the fairies' dearest playmates because of their vast imaginations. On warm summer days, they loved to lie on their backs, gazing at the clouds and shouting out names for the shapes they saw there. Then at night, they would lie in the same spot, admiring the constellations and whispering out names for the patterns they saw there. These two whimsies, which still entertain and intrigue us today, were both dreamed up by Cyclopes as innocents.

It is a mystery for you to solve that, as the Cyclopes became older, their terrific vision and sensitive character became too much for them to bear. So they slashed their sight and made themselves half-blind, and they froze their hearts and made themselves numb. The fairies, being loyal friends, offered again and again to help the giants correct their vision and bring back feeling to their deadened lives. But the fairies were always refused, and, of course, the Cyclopes could not be forced into correction and betterment. After a while, the fairies gave up. When that happened, Mother Nature lost patience and kicked the Cyclopes out of Earth and into outer space.

Which may not have been a wise thing for Mother Nature to do. Because you surely remember what happened before when other unenlightened types were forsaken and left to their own devices. How Earth was invaded, and things got messy and have been messy ever since.

Yet, what is done is done. We will not speculate any further about the consequences here. Although I will add Mother Nature does regret turning the Cyclopes loose and has promised never to make the same mistake again. These days she fights fire with fire. So we best behave ourselves and treat Earth with respect and insist others do the same. Particularly pitiful giants.

After the massacre of Pennsylvania's hemlocks and white pines, new trees came to settle and grow throughout the state, including Lightfall Hollow. Not without conflict, however. The new trees that arrived first resented the new trees that came later, and those new trees resented the new trees that came even later than they. And thus it went. It was silly. As Father Time tried to tell the trees, in his old gray eyes, the passage of a few hundred years is not even a blink. "You're all newcomers," declared Father Time.

But the trees did not see it that way. There was lots of discrimination from the new trees toward the other, newer trees in terms of access to land and other resources. The Stone Harvesters have told me my best tree friend in Lightfall Hollow, Wilton Weeping Willow, had it particularly hard because he comes from a foreign country. In addition, Wilton's looks are considerably different from the other trees. Even his color is different. Yet, it is hard for me to imagine anyone objecting to Wilton as a neighbor. For a tree labelled a crybaby, he could not be less of a whiner. He is pleasant to be around, gives more than he takes, and all that he really wants is what we all want, a place in the sun. While his silvery-green color is to die for.

The prejudice finally ended after Mother Nature put her foot down and permanently fixed the trees in their place. Because before Mother Nature gave them a time-out, on the night of any snow blizzard, when humans prefer to stay indoors and the world outside appears fuzzy and blurred, trees were free to walk, run, skip, and dance. That liberty ended when Mother Nature taught them a lesson, the lesson of what it feels like when beings are not free to ever move and be where and how they want to be.

Now the trees stay put. Even during the most blinding blizzard. Like I said, woe to them who overly provoke Mother Nature.

It is such a shame for the trees. Because the fairies have told me how much the trees enjoyed walking, running, skipping, and especially dancing. Many of our human dances were inspired by trees via their fairy dust being sprinkled on the feet of the right people. The hokey pokey, cha-cha slide, ballet, tap, macarena, chicken dance, waltz, limbo, breakdance, and more were all first performed by trees at night in a snow blizzard. The trees were supreme dancers too. Second to none. Sorry, people. Although the trees did cause soil erosion with their boogieing. So I guess there is a silver lining to this story.

Absolutely good news is the trees have made a lot of social progress while in time-out. They are some of Earth's best sharers now and their communities are some of the most integrated. They welcome all new trees with open branches. Moreover, with the help of their thread-like fungal friends, the mycelium, they connect their roots with the roots of their fellows. The result is a network for the fair distribution of resources among an entire tree neighborhood.

Despite the erosion issue, which everyone agrees will have to be resolved, the fairies hope someday soon Mother Nature will see fit to end her time-out. And I, Dusty Wonders, hope so too. Because by best tree friend, Wilton Weeping Willow, loves to dance, and he misses dancing immensely. Almost as much as he misses his significant other.

Wilton is head-over-heels in love with an oak tree who lives about a mile down the hollow. Her name is Olga Olinda, Ol-Ol for short. She is an old, weather-beaten thing who looks like she might flop over dead at any moment, but she always smells of buckwheat honey, so she must be sweet and still have a lot of life left in her.

Obviously, while in time-out, Wilton and Ol-Ol have been

unable to get together for even a brief stroll down lovers' lane, let alone dance. This has been particularly hard on Wilton. He spends his days longing to woo Ol-Ol once again with his cool breakdance moves and perfect pirouette. He aches for another chicken dance, cha-cha slide, or hokey pokey with Ol-Ol by his side. While his lonely nights are filled with dreams of waltzing his darling up and down the hollow.

For the sake of Wilton, Ol-Ol, the fairies, and me, I wish upon every star Mother Nature decides before long that enough is enough and allows trees to again uproot on pitch-black nights when the wind howls and snow flies in wild abandon. Because, even if I only get to watch through a window, and even if the scene before me is fuzzy and blurry, I would love to see Wilton breakdance, and I would love to see him take Ol-Ol in his willowy arms and waltz the night away. That sure would be something worth seeing all right.

Chapter Twelve

NESSIE AND PLUM

*A*S YOU now know, Lightfall Hollow is the business location for the manufacture and distribution of fairy dust. But this little woodland valley also serves as a retreat for magical creatures. Meaning any magical creature who at any time needs some relaxation, fun, fellowship, or sometimes it is privacy or even protection that is needed, is welcome to come to the hollow where they are given what they need for as long as need be, free of charge.

As you can imagine, with such an open invitation and lodging policy, Lightfall Hollow gets a thousand-and-one interesting guests. The Stone Harvesters have had the pleasure of hosting every type of magical creature from A to Z, from the Abominable Snowman of the Himalaya Mountains to Ziz, the great bird of ancient Israel, and once the Sandman spent his entire autumn here. Which made for a few restless months for most of the world, but we in the hollow got the best sleep ever that fall.

The first magical creature to seek retreat in the hollow was a dragon named Nessie. Nessie had once been a permanent resident here. Back when she was a new bride, she and her husband, Logan, had immigrated to Pennsylvania from Scotland. They settled in Lightfall Hollow, and for thousands of years, together they enjoyed a peaceful, loving, and meaningful existence.

When the first humans arrived in the hollow, it was Logan and Nessie who provided them with fire, something people had not had before. The humans were grateful for the dragons' gift. Most of Pennsylvania was a tundra back then. The weather temperatures were low to extremely low most of the year, and although there were plants like grasses, mosses, fungi, and shrubs, the land was almost entirely treeless, and the few trees that were here were short, little things. There was nothing to break the wind.

So, yes, as you can imagine, the humans were grateful for the dragons' gift. Now, no matter how freezing the elements, they could keep warm and cozy. The humans also found fire useful for cooking. Especially since it made many foods taste a lot better.

Logan was so pleased with his helpfulness to humans, he reckoned fire might prove handy to other creatures living on this land at that time too. So one Friday morning, while Nessie was out having breakfast with her Pegasus lady friends, Logan invited a herd of wooly mammoths, another of reindeer, and a pair of saber tooth tigers, along with their six cubs, to a fire demonstration. He assumed the animals would react like the humans had reacted. That their curiosity would outweigh their instinct to run from something new and different, and they would reach for the fire and learn to put it to productive use. But the mammoths, reindeer, and tigers ran, and the tundra caught fire. Logan had to sacrifice himself to put it out, throwing his clammy reptile body on acres upon acres of burning grass and shrubbery until at last the fire was smothered within his loving embrace. Although by that time, Logan had been fried to a crisp.

Nessie took Logan's death extremely hard. Heartbroken and self-accusing, she returned to her native Scotland to be near family. But even with the support of her relatives, Nessie's grief was so deep she could not climb out of it. Turning her back on all she had been, she became the Loch Ness Monster, vowing to spend the rest of her days in a lonely, bottomless lake, keeping her own fire doused and of no harm. The Stone Harvesters have told me Nessie believes she is making the world a safer place. However, even though the fairies pity poor Nessie, they do not agree with what they see as the cowardly waste of a great and natural gift. So, I am just wondering, what is your opinion of Nessie?

For all her anguish and putting herself down, Nessie has never stopped loving Lightfall Hollow. Her happiest memories are here, and this is where she finds some measure of relief. The high hope among the fairies is someday Nessie will also find peace. Not in Loch Ness and not even in Lightfall Hollow. But where it really counts. Within herself.

When Nessie first sent word from Scotland, asking if she might temporarily return to the hollow for a bit of a break, the Stone Harvesters responded with an enthusiastic "Yes!" Since then, Nessie comes back here every summer. But she always keeps to herself, staying hidden in the pond Logan dug with his talons for her luxurious bubble baths, as well as the couple's romantic swims on moonlit nights.

During Nessie's visits to Lightfall Hollow, many a fairy and other magical creature have tried to reach out to her, but, with one exception, she always refuses the good will. (You might ask why Nessie's Pegasus lady friends are unable to console her. Well, the reason is, by the time Nessie returned to the hollow, the winged mares had flown off to places mysterious and un-mapped. Which, of course, is their grand purpose. So please do not go blaming the Pegasi for not being there for Nessie. In their hearts, I am sure they are and will always be.)

When I was ten years old, I myself once tried to befriend Nessie, thinking a human buddy might be just the ticket. Howbeit, secretly, I was also assuming our being friends would get me a dip in the pond with Nessie. Although I had not yet learned to swim because I was too afraid to try, I had it in my head being pulled through the water while holding on to the neck of a dragon turned lake monster would be way cool. Even cooler than being dragged around via a dolphin fin or pushed along by a manatee's snout. But I never got to find out. Because the only thing I received from Nessie was a surprise dunking when a stray blaze of her breath punctured the raft I had paddled out on, and it deflated, and down into the pond I went. As I surfaced, gasping for air, Nessie was nowhere to be found. Down I went again. Luckily, a mermaid saw me drowning and saved me. So I learned a lesson. Fire-breathing dragons turned lake monsters do not make very good lifeguards.

The only one in Lightfall Hollow who has ever been accepted by Nessie is the Stone Harvester, Plum Purple. Plum is a descendant of Mountain. He is the son of Mauve and Mulberry. Although he did not start out that way. Before he knew better, Plum was Lilac, Mauve and Mulberry's daughter and the sister of Violet. But Plum figured things out, and parted ways with Lilac to be Plum.

For some reason, Plum has a way with Nessie. She opens up to him and talks freely. I know this because, on many an occasion, I have eavesdropped and spied on the two of them together. Although I do not understand dragon language, and I do not understand lake monster language either, I hear the relief in Nessie's voice as she goes on and on while Plum quietly listens.

Sometimes Nessie breaks down in hot tears, hanging her head and openly sobbing as Plum gently rubs her bowed neck. Then there are the times Nessie rests her head on Plum's shoulder and sighs. Which is probably not so great for Plum since Nessie's head is about a jillion time bigger than Plum's whole body, and she risks catching him on fire with exhalations like that.

Even so, it is obvious Nessie and Plum are fantastic friends, and just last week I heard and saw something I had never heard or seen before. It was Nessie and Plum, and they were cracking up together, laughing. Nessie's belly guffaws made for one big sweltering wind blowing through the hollow, but I did not mind the heat and humidity and my dripping sweat. Because I know a miracle when I hear and see one, and Nessie and Plum's laughter is a miracle.

Chapter Thirteen

CLOVER AND CRICKET

SPEAKING OF miracles has reminded me to finally get around to telling you about the Stone Harvesters, Clover and Cricket. Sister and brother, they are also fraternal twins. Both came into this world with bodies unusually tiny and frail. Likewise, they arrived with wings too underdeveloped and weak to fly.

Initially it was assumed the siblings would outgrow their physical impairments. However, they did not. The disabilities were permanent, and there was nothing anyone could do about that.

Since the two could not fly, they could not travel the universe, collecting remembering rocks and witnessing the marvels of the cosmos like the rest of their tribe. Nor did they have the muscle to work at the fairy dust mill, grinding stones and singing their hearts out together with their friends. These hard facts, along with the seeming pointlessness and loneliness of it all made the twins bitter and difficult.

They chose their names, Clover and Cricket, not as homage to the strong, Jolly Green Giant green of summer and the bright, Jiminy Cricket green of spring, but as a kind of angry, resentful, sarcastic joke of which they were the butt. Since both the plant and insect are thought to bring good luck, and Clover and Cricket felt they had been sent nothing but bad luck. Still, as luck would have it, upon naming themselves, just like the wings of every other Stone Harvester, their own wings took on the colors of their choosing, and it was those colors of their choosing that brought good fortune to Clover and Cricket once and for all. To say nothing of the good fortune it delivered every creature on Earth, magical and non-magical alike.

It all began to come about when Clover and Cricket's chosen greens got them noticed by the little green-glow alien kids. The extraterrestrials had recently arrived in Lightfall Hollow as refugees after their native planet was destroyed by a gang of murderous giants. No more than children, the youngest generation of their ancient species, they were tiny little things, much smaller than your average fairy. They had penguin-like wings that were useless for flying (having become unneeded during the aliens' evolution) and skin that alternately glowed with the same strong and bright greens as Clover and Cricket's wings.

The aliens felt drawn to the twins. The familiar greens provided the first bit of attraction. Then there were the additional similarities in both body and wing. But what finally made the affinity too strong to resist was the exact same loneliness. It was their mutual loneliness that moved the little green-glow alien kids to try to befriend Clover and Cricket.

Which was a humongous chunk of good luck. Because the fairy twins and the alien kids had one other thing in common. They had minds that were open, curious, imaginative, creative, and strong. The green-glows already knew this about themselves, but Clover and Cricket had no idea how gifted they were until the aliens taught them

At first, Clover and Cricket wanted nothing to do with the extraterrestrials, and they ignored all invitations for friendship. The twins had become that hurt and withdrawn. Yet, it was not long before the scientific experiments the aliens regularly conducted lured them in. They could be so exciting and really rather marvelous too. Particularly the ones that ended in loud explosions, shatterings, and leaping, out-of-control flames.

Although the absolute favorite was the one that turned the water in Nessie's lake monster pond into a gross, giant glob of hot pink goo. That one had the twins clapping their hands in glee and jumping for joy. Which was quite something. Since Clover and Cricket had never before known, much less shown very much happiness.

On the other side of the story, poor Nessie. The goo stuck to and between her dragon/lake monster scales like bubblegum would to your hair. She had to fly to the North Pole and submerge herself in the Artic Ocean's ice until the goo froze, and she could pick it off, a process that, given the sharpness of Nessie's talons and the slowness of her chilled reptilian body, was painful and took no less than two weeks.

If that were not miserable enough, Nessie came down with a severe cold and cough and was so full of congestion she could not fly herself back to the hollow. She had to be airlifted out of the North Pole by a herd of resident reindeer who were more than a little perturbed when Nessie's coughing fits singed their fur and left unattractive black holes in their precious coats. Nor did they appreciate it when Nessie's ears kept popping during the flight, shooting out smoke thicker than a December fog, making it impossible for the reindeer to see, as well as causing them to cough even harder than Nessie. They kept losing their way and, at one point, ended up in the Himalaya Mountains where they suffered various injuries, like bent antlers, nose bleeds, cracked teeth, and black eyes, all from bumping face-first into tall peaks.

I guess that is why, upon arrival in the hollow, the reindeer dumped Nessie off in the pond the way they did, dropping her from ten thousand feet and not even waiting to see if she had safely splashed down, zooming away without so much as a fare thee well. It all turned out okay though. Because Nessie landed unharmed, and after two more weeks of nose blowing and hacking up green phlegm, she was in good health again. Although ever since then, the pond has had a trace of a snotty tinge.

But back to Clover and Cricket and their initiation into the world of science. Since the magical world had yet no knowledge of science, the twins did not realize what the little green-glow alien kids were conducting was purposeful, orderly research. To them, the trials and tests the highly advanced extraterrestrials performed looked like amateur attempts at magic gone woefully wrong. Even though Clover and Cricket's perceptions were not exactly correct and even though they took impish delight in all the apparent goofs, as they watched the aliens struggle with success, the twins grew to feel sympathy too. Thank goodness. Because it was their sympathy that gave Clover and Cricket more than enough in common with the aliens to change their minds and become friends. Which they did. And thank goodness again. Because it was their friendship that awarded Clover and Cricket the opportunity of a lifetime and their life's purpose and work.

I bet you have already guessed what I am going to tell you now. Clover and Cricket, under the excellent tutelage of the little green-glow alien kids, along with a lot of hard work, became scientists. Both proved to be brilliant in their field. Even the green-glows, crackerjack scientists themselves, said so.

No surprise there. As I told you before, the twins had minds that were open, curious, imaginative, creative, and strong. Long before the aliens had entered their lives, it was their practice to ask lots of questions about all the countless things that caught their interest and made them wonder, and their questions made them more and more observant. In addition, Clover and Cricket kept a record of their observations. That way they were always handy to be studied again and possibly connected to other observations. Which got the twins to having ideas. Many of which were wrong, but at least they had them, and their brains grew ever stronger.

Now certainly that is not all there is to being a scientist. Clover and Cricket still had a long way to go. But they had made themselves an excellent beginning, and the aliens helped them to move forward from there, teaching the twins everything they knew and including Clover and Cricket in on the scientific discoveries they had been working on since their arrival on Earth.

As the twins learned science, the alien kids dived into the enchantment of life on Earth. They reveled in its natural magic and loved it here, but they had come from a planet significantly different from ours. It was a place where the weather and light were always that of a lovely, moonlit summer night in the hollow. The green-glows suffered in the chill of fall, winter, and spring, comparative brightness of most days, and various precipitations here, and it was feared their long-term health might be at risk. So, eventually, with the blessing and best wishes of the magical world, they took off in their spaceships to search the universe for new living quarters more like their birthplace. Which, by and by, they did find. Hopefully, their new planet will never come within sight of those hateful killer giants.

It was soon after the aliens' departure that what can best be described as an evil spell descended upon the world. No one ever did find out where it came from. Some blamed the giants and feared Earth was next to be destroyed, but the giants' guilt was never proven, and, obviously, Earth was not destroyed. Although we came close. Here is what happened.

Slowly at first, and then with increasing speed, all of Earth's magical creatures lost their magic. When magic vanished, its creatures lost their purpose. Since there was no longer any reason to get up in the morning, the entire population went into hibernation deep underground. But the agony of living in idleness, emptiness, and isolation was too much for many to bear. A great number died. However, by no means all. The vast majority hung on, hugging hope.

As for the human world, without the workings of the magical world, it too suffered. Although no humans ended up dying, for people as well life became a lot less worth living. Because when magic departed, it took with it its partner, wonder, and so the world became only depressing.

For example, when the gnomes, who are the wonderworkers of all plant life, lost their magic, although flower gardens continued to exist, their blossoms were only dull, droopy things with no color, scent, graceful design, or glad bearing. Likewise, farm fields still yielded, but their crops were only bland, mushy things with no flavor, texture, or smell. The same kind of thing happened to every plant food or plant-based food there is, from apples and oranges to chocolate, cake, potato chips, and popcorn. Without the gnomes and their magic, these eatables and so many more lost everything that makes eating them fun.

Worse, when the nymphs, the wonderworkers of lands and waters, lost their magic, the forests, mountains, rivers, seas, and so forth no longer had what it takes to inspire painters, poets, musicians, and the like. Since the muses also lost their magic, their influence vanished too. Art became a forgotten thing, and humanity went numb.

You may think it good the trolls and gremlins lost their magic, but nothing could be further from the truth. Not many people know this, but trolls are the wonderworkers of not only bridges, but all architecture. Similarly, gremlins are the wonderworkers of machinery. So trolls and gremlins also inspire. Plus, they keep us on our toes. Which, I'll admit, comes by way of some pretty annoying mischief and even some nastiness every now and again. Nonetheless, the trolls and the gremlins are the ones who push builders to ever build better and better. It was disastrous when they lost their magic. Structures collapsed, and machines went kaput. The human world came to a standstill.

Hobgoblins are another group of hard-working helpers who do not get the recognition they deserve. They are the wonderworkers of homemaking. When they lost their magic, all residences became filthy, chaotic, gloomy, and uncomfortable places. Humans no longer had a safe space for their hearts to reside.

As for the fairies, of course they also lost their magic. They could no longer help Mother Nature with her work. An overwhelming burden was now on her shoulders alone. Mother Nature tried, but there was no way she could manage without her most able assistants. Nor could she cope with the loss of so many of her magical children. Her heart grew so heavy she could no longer do her job. Life on Earth was in grave danger of dying.

How lucky it is then that Clover and Cricket came to the rescue. Those two scientists got to work right away, and they refused to stop until they found a cure and made magic real again. It took a lot of trying, and they made a lot of mistakes, and they had to endure a lot of suspicion, criticism, and unpleasantness from those whom they were laboring to help.

Even more exasperating during their fight to save the world was that the twins sometimes disagreed with each other. On a few occasions, the arguments between them overheated and spun out of control. Both said things they later regretted.

But Clover and Cricket were no strangers to frustration and anxiety. It was their bad luck to have known those two conjurers of unhappiness up close and personal for all of their lives. Now, however, what was once a misfortune favored them with patience and charity for others and themselves as well.

Well-provided for then, the two scientists kept at it, and eventually they succeeded in defeating the evil spell that had befallen the world. Magic became real once again. And along with magic returned wonder. Afterwards, Papa Space, who, as you may have already gathered, has a weakness for awarding titles, hailed Clover and Cricket "Master Magicians." Which, although the magical world was grateful to the twins, raised quite a few eyebrows among its creatures (including even those with no eyebrows), who worried about where such an association could lead.

A formal complaint was issued to the elders. It was Father Time who resolved the matter by proclaiming magic and science twins, not identical by any means, but born from the same source. "A source," he said, "that is also a hope-filled dream." And I have a hunch you know what that source is without my telling you. Because it is your superpower, the one that Gold especially admired.

Five hundred years have passed since Clover and Cricket saved the world with science. They still cannot fly or strive in the fairy dust mill like the rest of the Stone Harvesters, but the twins continue to work wonders with their own kind of magic. Although, while meaning no disrespect to Papa Space, they never think of themselves as having attained the rank of Master Magicians. Instead, they invariably aim to be devoted servants for the common good. Which is not only noble, but personally wise of Clover and Cricket, since it gives them more space for continuing fulfillment. Their lives are ever satisfying. They are happy. They have many, many friends, and their influence is far-reaching.

Indeed, there is a rumor that persists to this day in the magical world that it was Clover and Cricket's impact upon Earth that sparked the scientific revolution of the 16th and 17th centuries that brought modern science to the human world. When the twins are asked if this is true, they always reply, "Good heavens, no." Then they look up to the sky and smile mysteriously.

So, I wonder.

Do you?

Chapter Fourteen

BOOGEYMAN

*A*LTHOUGH I do often wonder at it, if there is one thing I never doubt, it is how wonderfully lucky I am. Lucky to have as my friends Luna Shadow, Gold, Plum Purple, Clover, and Cricket, along with so many other Stone Harvesters, fairies, and magical creatures. I cannot imagine my life without them. I love them so much. I can't ever lose them.

Not that there is any chance of that ever happening. Not when I have reams of their stories yet to tell. Why, come to think of it, apart from Nessie, I have not even begun to give you the low-down on the many magical creatures who, while not permanent residents, visit Lightfall Hollow on a regular basis and whose stories I have come to know. Honestly, at this rate, it will take me forever to get to the end of all their fairytales.

This does not mean, however, that I think I should keep my nose to the grindstone every single moment. It is always important to take some time for fun. Even Luna, my old, super-demanding task-master, thinks so. Which, I suppose, is why she is insisting I come to the party the Stone Harvesters are throwing tonight. She says there will be no excuse for my not being there. But, oh, for crying out loud, give me a break! I adore Luna, but she can be far too bossy.

Not that I don't want to go. I do. But I am an old lady now, and lately I have been feeling tired, and the Stone Harvesters, like all fairies, are always throwing parties. I have already been to a gazillion of them, and there will always be another. What is the big deal if I miss this one?

On the other hand, a good many of my closest magical friends from outside the hollow just happen to be visiting right now and will be there tonight. Luna says even Boogeyman has promised to show up. Which is surprising since there is no one more painfully shy than Boogeyman. Despite the fact he is frequently a guest at Lightfall Hollow, it has taken me decades and lots of trying to get to know him. But I have gotten to know him, and there is no one I respect, admire, and want to be like more than Boogeyman. He is my hero.

The reason Boogeyman comes here so often is to seek sanctuary from the pursuit of bounty hunters who are after the fat reward for his capture and murder, offered by those who were told, as children, fibs about Boogeyman and, as grown-ups, still believe he is a bad guy who should be brought to justice. But Boogeyman is not a bad guy. He is a good guy.

He is scruffy looking. His hair is stringy, dirty, and tangled, and his clothes are rumpled, ripped, and filthy. His face and hands could use a good scrubbing too, and I suppose there are people who would find disgusting the crusty blob of gray snot beneath his nose that is always there.

Probably just as objectionable to some, Boogeyman is not all that great at being sociable and practicing the social graces. His speech is rough, and his manners could use a proper polishing too. However, if you were made homeless, dragged through the mud, and had your reputation torn to rags so that generations of children were made scared to death of you, you too would probably be unkempt and not try all that hard to be charming and fit into polite society.

Hope you are now curious as to how Boogeyman got such a bad rap. Because I am about to tell you. It all began in England during medieval times when Boogeyman was a scarecrow standing in a farmer's field of crops. He certainly was not the first scarecrow in our world. However, in England during the Middle Ages, he was fairly unique. Since there and then scarecrows were not typically used to guard crops against birds and other hungry wildlife. Instead, it was the common practice among farmers to have their young children protect the fields, a duty that continued at all hours of both day and night.

However, this one farmer was both a rather tender fellow and a habitual worrywart. This was especially true when it came to his three little boys and three little girls. Adding to his apprehension for his kids was that, a couple of years back, the children's mother, his dear wife, while on errands in the nearby village, was senselessly attacked and murdered. Consequently, the farmer hated the thought of his children being out of his sight and beyond the safety of their home, vulnerable to all kinds of who knows what evil.

So early one spring morning, the farmer took a pair of his old, worn-out pants, along with an old, worn-out shirt, stuffed them with straw, and joined them together with a belt of grape vine. Next, he got a big, round gourd, smeared a face upon it with clay and charcoal and added hair from the shaggy ends of his oxen's tails.

The farmer jammed a stick horizontally through the shirt's arms, stretching them wide open. He attached the head to the body with another stick jammed vertically through the center of both and carried the finished scarecrow out into the field. There, he lashed it to a stake with strong rope and called to his six children to come meet their new servant.

The children came running. They looked over the scarecrow and declared him a dummy and a bum. Which incited five of the six to take turns kicking the scarecrow's threadbare shins and punching his belly of straw. They stopped though when the youngest sibling among them, little Beatrice, began to cry and beg mercy for the scarecrow. Which led Nash, the eldest sibling, to comfort his little sister by picking her up and holding her close to the scarecrow's face.

"There now, Beatrice," soothed Nash. "Kiss his cheek, and you'll make it all better." Which the little girl tried to do. But she missed and instead kissed the scarecrow right beneath his nose, leaving, not only a kiss, but a booger from her own nose. You might think Beatrice was embarrassed when she saw what she had done, but she was too young and innocent for that. Instead, she laughed and declared, "Boogeyman. His name is Boogeyman." And just like the booger, the name stuck.

Things went along okay for several years after that. Boogeyman was good at his job, and the farmer's field yielded an abundance of crops. While his six children grew and flourished too.

But the same could not be said of the farmer. The older he got, the more of a worrywart he became. He worried, worried, worried. Worried so much he ended up worrying himself sick. He became overly protective of his children. He kept his kids always with him. He did not grant them any space. He watched with fear and foreboding everything they did and tried to control their every move. If any one of them ever did manage to get a hold of a little freedom and privacy, he would freak out and make that child feel bad about themselves.

Given the loss and loneliness the farmer suffered, his actions were forgivable, but they were also hard to bear. There came a time when the kids, with Nash as their leader, decided they just could not take it anymore and should leave. So, one night, during the wee hours, the six siblings slipped out of their home and headed for London, where Nash assumed they were certain to make their fortune.

Though forgivable too, it was a terrible thing the children did to their father. The farmer was left without a clue as to where his children might be and what may have happened to them. He imagined the worst, and it drove him crazy. And I mean really crazy.

He blamed Boogeyman. Which was crazy. But, desperate for someone to be responsible for his nightmare, frantic for some sort of answer, the farmer in his pain and madness made himself believe Boogeyman was bewitched.

"Bewitched," he said, "obviously bewitched by the crows who, as everyone knows, are the cohorts of witches. Bewitched, so as to murder and feed to the wicked crows and evil crones my sweet angelic children."

With such language, the farmer spread his gossip. As gossip usually does, especially the absurd and slanderous kind, the farmer's story about Boogeyman grew by leaps and bounds and spread far and wide. So much so that it exists even today, seven hundred years later.

But now you know the truth. The gossip about Boogeyman is a lie. Further evidence is what happened next.

The farmer had worked himself up into such a rage, he was going to burn the scarecrow alive. No matter that the scarecrow was not alive. Yet, here's the mysterious part. Just as the farmer was about to destroy him, Boogeyman did come to life. As to why and how, I do not know. There are just some things in this world that cannot be explained, and from what I do know, a scarecrow turning into a man is one of those things. Feel free to disagree with me, however.

A flock of crows flying overhead were the first to notice the change in the scarecrow. Maybe because the farmer had unjustly accused them of horrible things too, the crows swooped down to the field. With their beaks and claws, they tore the torch from the farmer's hand and ripped apart the ropes that bound Boogeyman, setting him free.

Boogeyman ran for his life then. But not for long. Because with his new consciousness came old memories, and the richest of Boogeyman's memories were that of the farmer's six children. Most treasured was the first. Because though it began with a beating, it completed with Beatrice's kiss and enduring mark of love.

Of course then, Boogeyman returned to the farm, looking for his children. Although, as you know, they were not there. The crows were there though, and while crows are not wicked, they are farseeing. They told Boogeyman the children were in London. The crows also related why they had gone there and that Nash had been mistaken in his assumption. They had not made their fortune and were now beggars living on the street, cold, starving, and vulnerable to all sorts of danger.

Boogeyman could not let that be. So off he went to London where, with some help from his crow buddies, he located his kids. Although at first rather shocking, awkward, and even a little creepy, it ended up the happiest of reunions. Granted, before it was all over, there was a lot of crying. Numerous apologies were included too. Especially on the part of the middle four of the six children who, whenever Nash and Beatrice were not looking, had continued to batter and abuse Boogeyman. Which I consider unpardonable.

However, I get it. Boogeyman is more forgiving than me. He accepted the children's apologies outright. Just shrugged his shoulders and said, "Shucks, kids. It's all right." And that was that.

Except, not really. Because when Boogeyman had shepherded the children back to their home, carrying a frail Beatrice in his arms and another ailing kid on his back, the children forgave their father. In return, the father forgave his children. Isn't it amazing how so many things in this life are contagious?

From then on, the farmer stopped clinging to his children and began practicing the difficult art of letting go of what you are most afraid to lose. He therefore became the most loving father a father can be, and his children grew up to be independent, self-confident, productive, and resilient.

While Nash learned his lesson too. He never again just assumed something. He always did his homework.

As for Boogeyman, of course he was welcome to stay with the farmer and his children as a cherished member of their renewed and improved family. But it was too late for that particular happy ending. The gossip had done its damage, and Boogeyman was doomed to a future of relentless persecution. Still, we can hope for a just conclusion.

In the meantime, regarding all the bad stuff that has and continues to happen to him, Boogeyman, although he still hurts, has never blamed anyone, and he forgives everyone. So we need not worry about him. Because, as I trust you will agree, Boogeyman has made for himself the most happily ever after that ever could be.

Chapter Fifteen

Unicorns, Beavers, and Ponies, Oh My!

THE ONE magical creature I have never met and who will not be at tonight's party is a unicorn. Which is disappointing. Because, of course, I would love to meet a unicorn. I cannot imagine a more glamourous creature. Our ever meeting is impossible though since unicorns no longer exist. They used to, but then one day the glamourous unicorns became plain old ponies, and they have been plain old ponies ever since.

Here is what happened. It all started when the unicorns took pity on some beavers whose lodge in Lightfall Hollow was swept downstream and flooded after the beavers' dam had burst. Although the dam had been well constructed, a monster thunderstorm had gotten trapped in the Allegheny Mountains, making it rain cats and dogs for an entire night, dooming the beavers' home.

The next morning, after the storm had passed, the unicorns came out of the pine grove where they had been taking shelter and saw their neighbors' misfortune. Being good fellow citizens, they pulled off their horns and bailed out the beavers' lodge so that any unruined building materials and household items could be salvaged. Afterwards, the unicorns were unable to reattach their horns.

Which was a life-changer. Since the unicorns' horns held their magic. Without their horns, the glamorous unicorns became plain old ponies.

Oddly lucky is the unicorns had lost their magic before, back during the evil spell that snuffed out magic until the fairy twins, Clover and Cricket, came to the rescue with science. Having had that experience, the unicorns-now-ponies knew for sure they did not want to go into hiding. It had been a waste of time before, and it would be a waste of time again. Besides, Clover and Cricket had proven magic does not only belong to the magical world. Magic is within reach of the plain old world too.

Realizing this heartening truth, the unicorns-now-ponies were able to call up the inner strength to accept and adjust to the big change in their lives. Helpful too was their understanding that glamour is not all it is cracked up to be. It tends to be high maintenance. Worse, it can hide what is beautiful.

Just like Clover and Cricket, the unicorns-now-ponies worked hard to discover and develop a new kind of magic. They succeeded too. I know this because, although I have never met a unicorn, I have met plenty of ponies, and they always share with me their magic to comfort and heal. To make better whatever is ailing me at the time. Especially when I scratch them on that spot on their forehead where their unicorn horn used to be.

Although please do not ever just walk up to a pony you do not know very well and begin scratching them under the forelock where their unicorn horn used to be. Or anywhere else either. Ponies can be temperamental. This is because today there are some ponies who are foolish enough to be bitter about their long-lost glamour. Perhaps someone should remind them of their noble heritage and that a plain old pony is a beautiful and magical thing. Wouldn't you agree?

The beavers were so awed by their friends' sacrifice, they tried to design their new lodge in the shape of a unicorn horn to commemorate what the unicorns-now-ponies had done for them. However, the task of drawing up a satisfactory blueprint proved too much for the beavers. Since beavers, although they are talented builders, have no architectural skills. Apparently, beavers are not very artsy. Try as they might, all their intended drafts of soaring triangular cones came out looking like dumped cow poop patties, and things were getting kind of depressing.

But then the rectangular pine trees from the next-door grove said they were willing to help. This was because the unicorns-now-ponies had been such considerate guests, and even though they were in the middle of coping with a challenging new development in their lives, they had been thoughtful enough to send the pine trees a little thank-you gift for the night they had spent with them during the storm.

The beavers eagerly accepted the pine trees' offer and were soon presented with the perfect master plan for a house in the shape of a unicorn horn. The beavers set to work constructing their new home and ended up with a lovely new conical lodge, the type of which their descendants still most commonly build today. Although it seems that modern beavers are a whole lot sloppier than their ancestors. Conical beaver lodges these days do not exactly resemble unicorn horns soaring to the heavens. At least not the ones I have seen.

I guess then it is a good thing the rectangular pine trees were so taken with their design they decided to copy it for themselves. So, every time you admire a Christmas tree, remember to thank unicorns, beavers, and ponies. And, of course, thank the conifer too. For though we trim its pine with glitz, the cone-shaped tree stands ever green for hearts humble and pure.

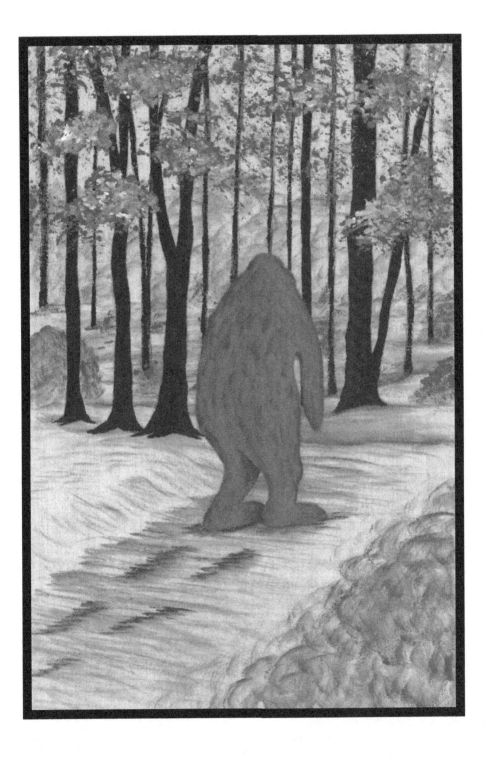

Chapter Sixteen

Baz and His Kin

THE FAIRIES were not the only magical creatures to observe and evaluate humans when we first began appearing on Earth. The sasquatches checked out and assessed us tenderfoots too. Like Gold, the most ancient and wisest of fairies, the sasquatches perceived a kinship with people. They saw us as members of the same family. For Gold, it happened as he watched children use their imaginations. For the sasquatches, it happened as they looked into human eyes and saw sasquatch.

Perhaps you do not know what a sasquatch is. Then does bigfoot perhaps ring a bell? Although I will tell you right now, sasquatches despise being called bigfoots. Which is totally natural. After all, who in the world wants to be told they have big feet?

There are many other names for the sasquatch species. All refer to huge, ape-like creatures who walk upright on two feet like we do and are covered with thick, shaggy hair. They live in secret in secluded wildernesses of all kinds throughout the world.

Since the end of prehistoric times, the sasquatches have been so successful at maintaining their privacy, there are now many people who do not believe they exist. Others feel certain, or at least think it is possible they do. Some of these individuals even go so far as to rove the most remote places on Earth, hunting for sasquatches, hoping to get solid evidence of their existence.

Yet, no one to date has been able to firmly establish that sasquatches are real. This is because they are magical creatures, and their powers allow them to elude their hunters. Not that they use glamour to hide. They do not. Because they do not need to. Rather, they use their ability to read minds and to communicate persuasively using only their minds. A sasquatch can read and direct the mind of any creature, including you and me. It is with these psychic powers sasquatches remain concealed from people.

I only happen to know for certain sasquatches exist because I am lucky enough to live in Lightfall Hollow where, needing a break from their isolation, sasquatches visit now and again to socialize with the Stone Harvesters and other magical creatures staying here at the time. And, boy, oh boy, do the sasquatches ever like to party and monkey around. I wish just once they would ask me to join them, but they have yet to do so, and I can understand why. A human to a sasquatch is an unwelcome invader of sasquatch privacy and maybe even a danger to sasquatch life and limb. It makes perfect sense that while the sasquatches are here, they all shy away from me. That is, all except Baz.

I am so thankful Baz trusts me and is never shy in my presence. We often get together when he visits Lightfall Hollow, and he is always free and easy and perfectly comfortable with me. I hope it is because when he looks into my eyes, he sees sasquatch.

In any regard, Baz is one terrific buddy. He gives even better piggyback rides than my father used to give. When we go hiking, and I get tired and think I can't walk another step, he just scoops me up with one arm and swings me onto his broad, hairy shoulders. Then we tramp on for miles and miles and miles. I'm telling you, I've seen a lot of beautiful country from atop Baz's shoulders.

He takes me swimming with him too. So I no longer feel like I missed out when Nessie failed to give me a ride in her dragon-turned-lake monster pond. I am proud to say that, even with me nervously clinging to his back and strangling his throat with my shaking hands, Baz does the world's finest cannonball.

And when my cat climbs a tree, Baz is so good about reaching up and bringing Ollie safely back down to earth and me. Ollie seems to really like the experience too. Afterwards, he purrs and purrs. Maybe that explains why more and more these days, my Ollie cat clambers up trees, only to meow from their branches for rescue.

Baz is also super helpful with the gardening around here. Although he is absolutely the worst at pulling weeds. He is way too heavy-handed and indiscriminate for that chore. Which I learned one early spring when he destroyed an entire field of my tenderly emerging and not-yet-in-bloom daisies and peonies. We had one heck of a fight over that disaster.

Yet, it is not too difficult for me to forgive Baz for his grossly incompetent weeding. Especially since he is second to none when it comes to harmlessly uprooting trees and replanting them where I say. As a result, my flowers and other plantings get just the right amount of sunshine and shade. Baz is also handy at yanking out heavy brush and heaving big rocks to clear more plots for my gardening, as well as getting his hands on enough water for my plants during dry spells. This he does by punching his fist down through the ground to the water-bearing rock of aquifers. People say I have a green thumb, but what I really have is a sasquatch.

I wish you too had your very own sasquatch. Hopefully, you will someday. Although not yet. Unfortunately, it looks like it will still be a while before sasquatches and people get back on speaking terms.

Which brings us to how sasquatches formed an amiable relationship with people during prehistoric times, why that relationship ended, and why sasquatches are not yet ready to befriend us once again. Except, of course, for Baz, who is as friendly and chatty as can be with me. We cordially yak it up together all the time.

I know from Baz it was the sasquatches who taught the first humans how to hunt animals for food. Without sasquatches, our species would not have survived its earliest days. Every single person on Earth would have starved to death, and you and I would not be here right now.

But the sasquatches did teach the rookie humans how to hunt, and they taught them fully and appropriately. They taught them to hunt with humble hearts and awed minds. They taught them to hunt with a deep appreciation and respect for the natural world and all its inhabitants. They taught them to never ever fail to thank the animals for their sacrifice and the gift of food. Food, not just for the survival of their human bodies, but also for the enrichment of their human spirits.

The first humans realized the sasquatches had saved their lives. They promised themselves, the sasquatches, and the heavens above to be eternally grateful and to always share the yields of their hunts with their big, hairy guardian angels. However, it did not take long for people to turn on their rescuers. They resented the sasquatches' enormous appetites and became stingy about sharing, poor behavior which the sasquatches accepted with good grace. Frankly, they had kind of been expecting it.

What the sasquatches had not at all anticipated was that humans would become so ungrateful and lazy they would begin murdering sasquatches to satisfy their own giant appetites. You see, the sasquatches were such large, easy targets, and the meat they provided lasted for months. So humans began murdering sasquatches. While sasquatches began using their psychic powers to escape humans, and they have been using their psychic powers to escape humans ever since.

Now I imagine you might be thinking it is high time for the sasquatches to get over the primitive past and give people a second chance. Because surely the sasquatches can see we humans have come a long way from wanting big, hairy apes for our long-term eating and health. Surely they can see that today we much prefer to stuff our faces and freezers with ice cream, popsicles, waffles, pizza, and cheeseburger sliders.

If indeed you are thinking that the sasquatches should just get over it, I must admit you have a point. Holding a grudge is most unwholesome. But I have gathered from Baz that sasquatch bitterness is not the problem. In fact, Baz says the sasquatches are eager to renew their friendship with our species. They hate living apart from us. It makes them lonely and sad. They miss us that much.

Which is amazing considering there is currently an additional reason for the sasquatches to shun us. It is the way some modern-day hunters hunt. With no humility, no respect, no appreciation, no gratitude, and certainly no awe. Hunters who hunt with a sense of entitlement. Who think they are the masters of Mother Nature. Who do not see the animals they hunt are fellow members of Earth's family and should be revered as the sacred creatures they are. Such hunters have closed their hearts and minds to the ancient ways, and they are an embarrassment.

On the contrary, there still are those hunters who do keep the ancient ways. Living here in the Allegheny Mountains of Pennsylvania, where hunting has a long tradition, I know this firsthand. Such hunters are worthy followers of the sasquatch ways, and the sasquatches are proud of them.

But, mind you, you don't have to be a hunter to have sasquatches be proud of you. These days, having opted to go vegetarian, there are sasquatches who no longer hunt. Anyone with humility, respect, appreciation, gratitude, and awe for Mother Nature's realm is worthy of sasquatch pride. If that describes you, you have the honor due you too because the sasquatches keep close track of you.

Although sasquatches live only in secluded places, they continually visit other locations, and I'm not talking about their travels to Lightfall Hollow. Using their psychic abilities, sasquatches remotely observe all things and happenings on Earth. This extrasensory perception of theirs is kind of like you watching television reality shows 24/7, except what the sasquatches see really is real and not just a dumb waste of time.

The sasquatches watch us humans with a constant eye, and Baz tells me they are more and more encouraged by what they see. Which, I know, can be hard to believe. It is so much easier to see that, in addition to some hunters, there are also many other people these days, like the Cyclopes of old, who don't care at all about Mother Nature and her environment. But Baz says to see only that is to see things all wrong, and that can make someone mean and too sad and discouraged to be of any help. That's why the sasquatches are always working to improve their own views of people, and lucky for both them and us, they are making good progress.

There is therefore reason to believe the day is coming when sasquatches will no longer hide from us. They will reveal themselves to those worthy of their trust, respect, appreciation, and awe. It will be their greatest achievement, and Baz says, "The sooner, the better. All this aloneness does no one any good. It keeps us small, and we are meant to be big."

I have to agree. Because sasquatches are the magical creatures closest to people. And you can take it from me. It really is something to look into sasquatch eyes and see human. Living proof of the marvels we are. An extraordinary yield of the hunt.

Chapter Seventeen

Willa's Ghost

I DON'T NEED to go to tonight's party to be with ghosts. Ghosts visit me whenever and wherever I choose. Like anyone else, all I must do is invite them.

In case you do not already know, ghosts are somewhat like remembering rocks, but more exclusive. What I mean is, unlike remembering rocks that get manufactured into fairy dust to become a part of everything, ghosts are specific to individuals. That is why, for any one person, the ghosts they summon are typically those of their friends and family. But such loved ones do not have to be the limit when it comes to having ghosts. Take me, for instance. I keep company with all sorts of ghosts. Any being I have ever felt a personal connection with is always welcome to haunt me, and therefore they do.

Not that I see ghosts. I do not. At least not in the usual way. Like the way I would see you if you were right here in front of me now. But you are not right here in front of me now, are you? Or are you? You could be. Because a ghost does not have to be a ghost of the dearly departed. A ghost can also be the apparition of a being alive in the physical world. All that is necessary to be a ghost is a spirit, and, of course, you have a spirit, and I trust you are constantly growing that spirit ever bigger and stronger.

In any respect, while it may be different for others, I do not see ghosts with my eyes. I do not hear with my ears what they say to me either. Nor have I ever touched a ghost with any part of my body or felt on my skin a ghost touching me. Can't say too I have ever smelled one with my nose or tasted one with my tongue.

The kind of contact I am trying to describe is more direct than what needs the help of the five senses. It happens when spirits are buck naked with nothing in between them. Most often it is called forth by want and need. While it is backed up by memories and imaginings. Despite what some may say, want, need, memories, and imaginings do not make ghosts fake. They make them real. As real as you and me.

For the longest time on Earth, ghosts did not exist. They did not exist because no being had yet realized bodies and spirits are separable, and where a body fails, a spirit can succeed. But that all began to change when Willa was dying.

Willa was a will-o'-the-wisp who lived in Lightfall Hollow about 150 million years ago. A wisp of thin, feeble, flickering, bluish-white light, she was barely an adult when her parents were accidentally trampled to death by a stampede of panicked dinosaurs who had lost their way in the wisps' swamp home and were spooked by the peculiar lights. Afterwards, with both mother and father gone, it was clear to Willa the responsibility to bring up her baby sister, Ella, was now all hers.

Willa was unhappy to have been shouldered with such a ponderous obligation which she had neither asked for nor expected, much less prepared for. She tormented herself with feelings of inadequacy, worrying she was not up to such a big job. Willa was scared she was not strong enough to foster another being, and her fear frequently made her impatient, too demanding, and harsh with Ella.

Yet, despite her fear and iron-fisted ways with her little sister, Willa was not without a heart, and she grew to love Ella with every breath of her being. She grew to care about her more than she cared about herself. In the end, Willa became a devoted parent. And that devotion to Ella made Willa an indominable spirit.

However, an indominable spirit does not come with an indestructible body. While Ella was still just a child, Willa contracted a disease from some nasty bacteria in their swamp's water. Back then, there was no way to treat such a disease, and Willa had to face the fact she was dying.

Her major concern though was not for herself. It was for her sister. Willa could not bear the thought of leaving Ella all alone in the world to fend for herself. With all the energy of her tenacious spirit, Willa committed to continuing to accompany her beloved through life.

It is always amazing what love, loyalty, and a will of iron can do. But never more so than in the case of Willa. Her body died young, but for the rest of her little sister's long life in the physical world, Willa haunted Ella, coming to her whenever she was called.

(By the way, that old, truthful expression, "Where there's a will, there's a way" was inspired by Willa.)

After Willa died, other beings caught wind of her ghost, and spirits have followed Willa's lead ever since. Now there are countless ghosts, and some of them exist because of you. Don't be afraid. They care about you more than they care about themselves. They are devoted to you. They will come when you need and want them. They will come with memories and imaginings. They will come and nurture you with their wills of iron and everlasting love.

Chapter Eighteen

THE ALLEGHANS

O MATTER how strong the spirit that endures, no physical being likes to die. We have a deep-rooted instinct to survive in bodily form. No doubt because there is much to be gained by living a mortal life in this fantastic world. Dying changes that, and to complicate the matter even further, we tend to be wary of change. Yet, there is no stopping change. Everything is always changing. This is the truth, and we cannot defeat it, but none have ever more stubbornly tried than the Alleghans.

The Alleghans were the most gigantic of all giants who have ever lived on Earth. The first of their tribe were born here in Lightfall Hollow, children of the Allegheny Mountains and the rivers who embrace them. Even though, being conscientious about the damaging effects of overpopulation, they kept their numbers reasonable, the Alleghans grew so big, and their lifespan was so long, they had to spread out beyond the Alleghenies. At their peak of earthly existence, they inhabited our entire planet.

Incidentally, this was back when the first fairies were getting their start as the Stone Harvesters. While there were still ages to go before there were humans like you and me. But the Alleghans had many similarities to humans. Just like with the sasquatches, we are closely linked.

The Alleghans were extraordinary beings. They were taller than the tallest mountain, stronger than the strongest river, and they had hair blonder than the blondest sun, eyes blacker than the blackest night, skin bluer than the bluest sky, and freckles in the same patterns as our stars' constellations. Unlike the Cyclopes, they were as loving as adults as they had been as children, and they performed many wonders.

The Alleghans could see in total darkness, and they could hear the voices of all the inhabitants in the entire universe. They understood and were fluent in all their languages too. Like the sasquatches, they could read minds. Even more impressive, they could read the most convoluted dream as though it were a clearly written story. Their sense of touch was so sensitive, they could feel colors, and they could smell and taste them too. Most amazing of all, the Alleghans could make themselves invisible, as well as lighter than the lightest feather, and travel to anywhere they wanted to go at a top speed faster than even the maximum speed of fairy wings. Which was lucky for everyone else on Earth. Since the giants would have trampled to bits everything in their path had they covered ground as their hulking, heavy-footed selves.

But the Alleghans were gentle giants. They would lend a hand to even the lowliest creatures, and they were so tender even the smallest creatures did not fear them. They enjoyed a fond attachment to all beings and accepted all beings as they were. More than anything, the Alleghans valued the creative force.

Which is probably why they were artists. Musicians and sculptors, each one of their creations was an exquisite and imaginative original. As musicians, among other triumphs, they wrote smash hits for the birds to sing, the bees to hum, multitudes of other insects to trill, the winds to whistle, the seas to roar, and certain rocks to chime.

As sculptors, they fashioned from clay both fanciful and realistic forms. They welded rocks together to make stone pillars, paths, walls, and mounds with secret chambers chiseled out beneath them. They whittled the bones of dead creatures into live images. They did the same with wood. Their masterpieces they molded from silver and gold into their own likenesses.

The Alleghans were some of the greatest creative geniuses our world has ever known. Yet, over time, they increasingly noticed something about everything they made. They noticed that, in the course of time, each work changed.

Musical pieces were adapted to better fit their latest musicians. Then they were passed down, only to be revised again and again until the original versions were no longer remembered. Clay sculptures fell apart. Stone structures crumbled. Images of bone turned to dust. Those of wood rotted to dirt or burned to ash. While the Alleghans' statues of themselves wore away until they looked like strange, unknown creatures.

Looking at the world around them, the Alleghans realized what was a reality for their creations was also a reality for everything on Earth. All things constantly changed. They changed and then, sooner or later, became something different. The giants suffered this fact as a terrible truth. It made their hearts sick, and they trembled and wept with a bitter longing for something that would never change and last forever as it had begun.

The Stone Harvesters tried to comfort the Alleghans. They listened with gigantic sympathy and wiped away giant tears with tissues of puffy clouds, cooled giant brows with mountaintop snow, stroked giant hair with rays of the sun, and patted giant backs with their little fairy wings. Just as generously, the Stone Harvesters shared what they thought would be encouraging news about their recently developed business enterprise. How they were beginning to manufacture fairy dust from remembering rocks to become a part of everything ever in existence. But the giants were not impressed. Nor were they comforted.

Father Time tried to cheer up the Alleghans as well. As I previously related, he has a rough time himself living with the temporary nature of all things within his realm. If Father Time had total command, he might be tempted to have things just go on and on and on the same way they began. But even Father Time must yield to a higher power, and to his credit, as painful as it is for him, he accepts the truth and goes along with it.

Still, Father Time had empathy for the Alleghans. He could feel their pain. Yet, the giants were no more moved by Father Time's efforts to hearten and comfort them than they had been with the fairies' attempts. You got to wonder why. The fairies' theory is the Alleghans, as grand as they were, and as good as they were to creatures less mighty, had never caught on even they had limits. For the first time, they were faced with something they feared they might not be able to beat.

One thing is for sure. The Alleghans were bound and determined to win, no matter what the cost. They were possessed by both their desire to achieve victory over their perceived enemy and their zeal to do so by any means necessary. Hence, they journeyed out into the sun's solar system, beyond what they thought were only the stupid limits of life on Earth. Their first stop was the moon, where they chiseled the image of a king upon its surface. But shortly thereafter some asteroids hit the moon, and their sculpture of royal highness changed to a simple face of a mere man. Undeterred, the Alleghans went on to Saturn and arranged the planet's rings into a bell choir that tolled to the tune of an imperial march. But soon the rings stopped playing the imperial march and began making their own kind of music. Then it was on to Pluto to carve its ice mountains into regal thrones. But in no time at all, glaciers overflowed the thrones and moved them down from their lofty seats.

The giants travelled out into our galaxy even further. Though they had no success anywhere else within the Milky Way either. Still defiant, they rambled around the rest of the cosmos. However, in this universe, there is no getting past Mother Nature, Father Time, and Papa Space. Everything the Alleghans did, no matter where they did it, always changed.

It took a while, but at length the Alleghans got it into their thick skulls that their venture had been a wild goose chase, and they had made laughable fools of themselves. If they had had any sense during that moment of truth, they would have enjoyed a good laugh and returned home. But the giants did not laugh, and they did not return home. Instead, they dug in their heels and roamed even further, past the orbit of sound judgement.

There was no place left to go but beyond the universe. So there the Alleghans went. It was a particularly twisted move. Since, at the beseeching of Father Time and the fairies, and because, unlike the Cyclopes, the Alleghans were not hurting anyone but themselves, Mother Nature had held back from cutting off all connection. But now the giants themselves let go of every relationship. Now not even the elders could reach them. They were on their own, beyond the universe, where there is nothing but nothingness.

For a few fading heartbeats, the giants were triumphant. Because one of the gazillion plus things that does not exist in nothingness is change. The giants got what they wanted. They got permanence. Although at the expense of no being at all.

Because, as you can understand, where there is nothing, there is no being. No thoughts. No feelings. No experiences. No stories. No growth. No grand honor of passing the torch to a bright new beginning.

The Alleghans were no dummies. In nothing flat, they changed their minds and hearts and wanted back their wonderful life on Earth. Despite its downside, the giants were ready to go home.

However, without the elders, the Alleghans had become disoriented, confused, and shaky. They did not know which way was Earth, and they did not remember how to become invisible and light, and they were too unsteady to be swift. For eons afterwards, they would be lost, stumbling about the nothingness, powerless and homesick.

Yet, even in nothingness, all is not lost. In the end and by some miracle, the giants did return home. But the nothingness and going so long without change and the growth change makes possible had taken its toll. As their feet touched Earth, the Alleghans died.

It was a peaceful death, filled with contentment. Afterwards, the giants' bodies were buried in the bellies of the Allegheny Mountains who had delivered them, embraced by the rivers who had sired them. If you care to look, you can still see their reposing frames in the gentle risings and fallings of the Alleghenies.

Needless to say, the Alleghans left behind remembering rocks which were then ground into fairy dust. No surprise there. What may surprise you though is that, despite their grave mistakes and wasting so much of themselves in nothingness, the giants' spirits endure. For within any creative impulse, there live the Alleghans.

Chapter Nineteen

Of Stardust and Seawater

ALL THINGS on Earth, yourself included, are made of stardust. Almost all the basic elements that comprise your body and everything else of substance on our planet had their beginning in the most ancient of stars. Those stars shone billions of years ago until they ran out of energy, exploded in a blaze of glory, and died. When the stars erupted, the elements they had generated were swept out into the universe as stardust. The stardust acted like seeds, and from them new stars grew. These new stars also produced elements. Then they too ran out of energy, erupted, died, and sowed their stardust to grow the next generation of stars. Thus, it went and continues.

But that's only the beginning. Over time, the elements of stardust also combine in different ways to make more things than just stars. Then those things combine to make other, more complex things. Ultimately, the elements get around to making things as complicated as Earth and you.

Stardust is like fairy dust. It's a connection to everything that ever was, is, and will be. It tells our story and keeps our existence ever in the past, present, and future. If you doubt this is true, look at the stars, and then try to fool yourself into believing you don't feel a connection. It can't be done.

It is much the same with Earth's water. Composed of the elements hydrogen and oxygen, more than half of the human body is made of water. Your brain and heart are over 70% water, and the blood coursing through you is over 80% water. Mixed with this water is salt, the greatest percentage of which is the same kind of salt, sodium chloride, most common in seawater and which is also present in all unprocessed water.

Just as amazing, the water here on Earth, including what is in you at this moment, has been here since the start of water on Earth. It just keeps getting recycled and will presumably continue to be recycled for as long as Earth exists. The water you slurp down today may once have been lapped up by the dinosaurs who stampeded through the swamp home of Willa and Ella's family. A snowflake you catch on your tongue this winter may once have been your mother's tear of joy when she first held you in her arms. A trickle of sweat you perspire this summer may some autumn be the drizzle that makes your father shiver. The vapor you exhale with your next breath may one day be a droplet in a rainbow that gives you hope when you need it most.

Water is another connection. It is an additional reminder the Stone Harvesters are right. We are all in this wonderful life together forever. If you doubt this is true, just look at an ocean, and then try to fool yourself into believing you don't feel a connection. It can't be done.

We are of stardust and seawater. It follows then everything we create is of stardust and seawater too. Within our works is connection to everything that ever was, is, and will be. Which is why our creations are so important. These include our stories. And not simply the real-life stories remembering rocks hold and fairy dust spreads, but also the stories we make up. For such works of imagination reach beyond our personal selves. They stretch to the heights of the stars and the depths of the oceans. As absurd as it is, such fictions leave truth behind to try to get to the highest and deepest truths. Sometimes they succeed too, and even if they do not, the journey they take is irreplaceable.

So I am grateful to the mermaids. Which is why I always thank them whenever they are here. Which, sadly, is not very often. Their profession keeps them so busy. But now and again, mermaids fly into Lightfall Hollow for some time off in Nessie's lake monster pond, arriving in stately fashion on the backs of griffins and phoenixes. They certainly deserve both the recognition and the R & R. Because it is the mermaids who ensure all whopper-loaded stories live on.

The story of the mermaids is another story of change and transformation, like the stories of Boogeyman, unicorns, Willa, along with so many other magical creatures and, if we are composing them correctly, the stories of our lives too. Because mermaids began as water nymphs called naiads, magical creatures from ancient Greece. The naiads' physical appearance was that of alluring young women with curvy figures, long, glossy hair that flowed in smooth waves, and eyes that boldly flashed beneath dark lashes. It was their job to manage Earth's fresh water sources, such as lakes, ponds, springs, and rain clouds. As if that were not enough, the naiads were also responsible for keeping watch over and protecting the young of our world. It was their favorite task, and they were pretty good at it too. That is, until one fateful day.

That day the naiads had been appointed guardians of a teenage girl named Persephone. Persephone's mother, Demeter, was a powerful magical creature, commanded by Mother Nature to train and supervise the gnomes in the art and science of agriculture. It was Demeter's responsibility to make sure Earth's soil was fertile and cultivated, farm crops grew, harvests were bountiful, and we humans were fed.

Demeter loved Persephone more than life itself, but her career was demanding, and she needed help from time to time with her daughter's care. Especially since Persephone was a born wanderer, prone to traipsing about the forest gathering and studying whatever wild and uncultivated plants she found there. You see, like a lot of children, Persephone was a bit of a rebel.

It probably would have been all okay though, except the naiads Demeter had assigned to protect her daughter that fateful day were as enraptured as Persephone by the exceptionally beautiful wildflowers they came upon during their wilderness wandering. You really can't blame them. The wildflowers were an intoxicating lot. They shone in the same dramatic colors as galaxies and oceans, and their glowing petals coiled in eye-popping whorls and cascaded in mesmerizing waves. While their sweet and pungent fragrance was life's own potent musk.

So you really can't blame the naiads for being distracted. Especially since the wildflowers had been watered by the rain and sparkled with the dew the nymphs directed. Theirs was a splendid accomplishment, and they simply forgot themselves in a moment of pride.

The naiads, along with Persephone, spread out in search of the most glorious of all those glorious flowers. Which is why Persephone ended up alone and unprotected. She was easy prey for the miserable, gone-bad-with-loneliness guy, Hades, and he kidnapped her.

Although it is a great story (and so famous it is easy to find if you are interested), we won't go much further here with the adventures of Demeter, Persephone, and Hades. Because, after all, this is the mermaids' tale, and we don't want to go astray by wandering too far into other stories. I will only add that the abduction of her darling daughter filled Demeter with the same overpowering, heart-slashing, and insanity-producing rage that would someday fill Boogeyman's farmer. It was the mad, blind fury of a parent with a child in danger and looking for someone to blame for that horror of horrors. A terrified, in pain, and deranged Demeter had no mercy for the naiads. She punished them by turning them into sirens.

You may not know what sirens are. So often these days they are confused with mermaids. However, though sirens and mermaids are closely related, they are not the same. In addition, sirens no longer exist. Quite some time ago, and in more than one way, they went the way of the unicorns. But when the sirens did exist, as magical creatures fabricated by Demeter, they had the same upper bodies as naiads, but from their bellybuttons on down, they were birds. In addition, sirens had wings attached to their backs. Yet, like now with penguins, the fairy scientists, Clover and Cricket, and the little green-glow alien kids, siren wings were useless, and sirens could not fly. Like I said, Demeter was without mercy when she turned the naiads into sirens for being so flighty with Persephone's care.

To further their punishment, Demeter threw the nymphs-now-sirens out of their fresh-water homes and sent them to a rocky, barren, deserted island in the middle of a narrow ocean channel connecting two seas. On the one side of this strait was a deadly whirlpool composed of clashing currents so strong they could sink ships. On the other side was a gluttonous sea beast with six heads on long snaky necks and crammed full of dagger-like teeth. For the sirens it seemed there was no way of escape.

But no one is ever without a way of escape. In the case of the sirens, they looked to the stars, and the stars told them everything they know. Which is everything, all there is to know in the universe.

But what to do with infinite knowledge? Especially when

stuck on a deserted island with few resources. Well, the sirens figured it out. Or at least they thought they did.

Demeter had prevented the sirens from being able to fly like a bird. Yet, in her mad, blind fury, she had forgotten birds are not only flyers, they are also singers. The sirens had inherited amazing singing voices, and within their song, they vocalized all knowledge.

We have now reached the place where this story gets ghastly for people. Even so, and despite what others have said, the sirens never meant our kind any harm. They merely wanted to share what they knew. With this as their desire, the sirens started singing their song of infinite knowledge to passing ships and the sailors aboard those ships.

As I would have predicted had I been around then, unlimited knowledge proved too much for the sailors to take in. Although I am confident we will get there someday, even now we humans are nowhere near to being able to receive all knowledge. Like I said before, evolution is a long, long voyage, and until we get to the awesome place to which we are headed, infinite knowledge blows human minds.

The sailors went crazy. They crashed their ships into the island's rocks and died. Not surprisingly, the shipwrecks and sailor deaths gave the sirens a bad reputation. And, truthfully, it is shocking it took the all-knowing sirens as long as it did to figure out what was causing the ships to crash upon their shores. I guess a bit of flightiness from their nymph days still lingered.

Meanwhile, back in ancient Greece, birthplace of the naiads-now-sirens, along came a man named Homer. Homer was a bard, an inventor and teller of long, far-fetched stories about the extraordinary deeds of extraordinary characters. Such fictions were in poetic verse and were known as epic poems. The bards shared them orally, by mouth, often singing them accompanied by a musical instrument called a lyre. It all made for dynamite entertainment. The people loved it.

For hundreds of years, the epic poems of ancient Greece were passed down from one generation of bards to the next. Each junior bard would revise the stories they had learned from the senior bards, changing the narratives to make them more their own. The constant revisions also kept the bards' performances fresh and interesting for their audiences.

Homer was perhaps the greatest bard of ancient Greece, and within his repertoire were two epic poems that were wildly popular with the public. Still hugely famous, today they are known as *The Iliad* and *The Odyssey*. Included in *The Odyssey* is a brief tale involving the sirens. It portrays them in a wicked light. They are seen as calculating murderers of innocent sailors. But now you know better because I told you the truth. Or at least I imagine I did.

Besides being an outstanding bard, the other remarkable thing about Homer was he was blind. I for one believe Homer's blindness made him both insightful and farseeing. That he saw stories for what they are. Of stardust and seawater, stories are living things.

If indeed Homer saw stories as living things, he would have

also seen every story has value. He would have seen stories must be cared for and protected. It is then reasonable to surmise it was Homer's seeing that gave him his astounding vision.

Homer's astounding vision was to write down *The Iliad* and *The Odyssey*, and it really was an astounding vision for three reasons. First, as I just told you, up to this point, for hundreds of years, a long line of bards had told their stories exclusively by way of the spoken word. Homer's idea was a radical break with a long-honored and well-loved tradition. We can only imagine how the other bards, as well as the general citizenry may have reacted. Secondly, although there already were a few other stories in the world that had been put into writing, a written story was still a newfangled idea, its worth questionable. Again, there was probably some backlash. Thirdly, braille had not been invented yet. Homer could not write. However, as we know from Willa's story, where there is a will, there is a way. Somehow, Homer got it done. Thank heavens.

And thank the heavens too for the sirens. Because being all-knowing, the sirens knew the same truth about stories as Homer apparently did. They also knew about Homer's astounding vision and his fulfillment of that vision.

Furthermore, being all-knowing, the sirens could see the future. They knew there would come times on Earth when, for one reason or another, certain stories would upset some people, and those people would try to prevent the stories that bothered and worried them from being told. Stories would be put in danger, in danger of losing their freedom and even their lives.

Like Homer, the sirens knew every story has value. They knew all stories deserve protection. And they were dying and willing to die to be the ones to provide that safekeeping.

The sirens differed with what they foresaw as people's misjudgment of certain stories, but they also realized that within those future human mistakes there might be a way to make amends for their own past mistakes. Even better, there might be a way to bring meaning and purpose back into their forlorn lives. Perhaps they could even regain the best of what had been theirs, guardianship of vulnerable, growing, and precious life.

The sirens asked the stars for help, but although stars are all-knowers and classic creators, they do not work unaided. "To put intelligence in motion," the stars advised the sirens, "you need the helping hands of the elders." With that, the sirens sang out with their amazing voices to Mother Nature, Father Time, and Papa Space.

The elders were as enticed by the sirens' song as any sailor had ever been. Fortunately, however, their superpowers are far superior to even the pull the sirens once had. Like they had helped the Stone Harvesters work out a plan to preserve all factual stories, the elders helped the sirens work out a plan to preserve all fictional stories.

The sirens knew that close to the island where they were stranded, deep beneath the ocean, there is a vast sea cave unknown to any human. It was then and still is unknown to any human because it is a magical sea cave and the source of all magic. It is the womb where magic began and is yet being created.

Although the cave is underwater, it has countless dry chambers. The sirens foresaw this sea cave remodeled into a secret library where all stories would be kept safe, free, and alive. As to how to acquire the stories for their library, over the centuries of their exile as lonesome half-birds, the sirens had reached out and gotten chummy with many a fine-feathered friend. The sirens knew all they had to do was ask, and flocks upon flocks of birds would eagerly agree to fly around the world, listening and committing to memory all stories being told.

Upon their return, the birds would sing the stories to the sirens who would then borrow Homer's vision. They would put each story down in writing, transcribing it and binding its pages together. The resulting book would be categorized with a proper identity and given snug sanctuary on a stone shelf in the cave library deep beneath the sea.

It was a good plan. The elders approved it with the same enthusiasm and for the identical reasons they had given a thumbs-up to the first fairies' plan. With every siren voting in its favor, the plan was adopted. All systems were go.

Well, that is, except for a few rather major details. For one, the sirens were still stuck on that blasted deserted island. But not for long. Because like she had done for the Stone Harvesters, Mother Nature came to the rescue. As she had instructed the fairies to get wings, she instructed the sirens to lose theirs and to replace their bird bottoms with fish bottoms. Which the sirens did. Just like that. Upon their transformation, Papa Space, with his never-ending obsession for naming things, declared the reborn sirens "young ladies of the sea who shall henceforth be known as mermaids."

The next problems to solve were where to get help transforming the dry chambers of the sea cave into a library, as well as ongoing assistance shelving books once the library was up and running. As you can easily imagine, mermaids cannot get around very well in waterless library rooms, and library rooms must stay waterless. (If you don't believe me about that, just ask any librarian.)

Once again, the mermaids' friends came through for them. And, in an odd way, so once again did Demeter's mad, blind fury. Because not only did Persephone's mother punish the naiads that fateful day, she also punished the wildflowers that had distracted the nymphs from her daughter's protection. She ripped every single one of the blooms out by their roots and cast them into the ocean, where they changed into sea elves.

Sea elves, like mermaids and frogs, are amphibians. They can breathe both underwater and above it. Unlike mermaids, however, sea elves have legs and can get around quite well in waterless libraries. Which they do by hopping about the same as frogs.

Like the flowers they come from, their passion is making the world a more beautiful place, and because they are elves, they are natural builders and artists. The sea elves eagerly went to work constructing spiral bookcases to wind from floor to ceiling in the mermaids' library, chiseling them from stone and carving them all over with every type of magical and nonmagical creature that has ever lived or will ever live.

The ceilings, walls, and floors of the library chambers the sea elves treated as gigantic canvases, creating abstract paintings in the same dramatic colors and textures of galaxies and oceans. As a final touch, the sea elves speckled their masterpieces with glittery minerals that made the paintings sparkle like a starry sky or a sun-spangled sea.

The effect was breathtaking, but a library needs more light than glitter can provide. A library needs sufficient light by which to read. (Again, just ask any librarian.)

So the sea elves called upon their aquatic buddies, and they too came swimming to help. Bioluminescent jellyfish, squid, sea stars, lantern fish, and lantern sharks arrived by the hundreds. They all gave their gift of light to light to reading perfection the mermaids' library. How wonderful it would be if all libraries had the resources to be illuminated by such warm, vibrant, and dedicated lamps.

The mermaids' library was complete. A library more superior has never existed. A supreme gift to humankind had been given.

Mermaids, again like fairies, are not immortal. All who were once nymphs and sirens are dead. Yet, their progeny flourish in ample number. A good thing too. Since at present there are a lot more stories to protect.

Devoted scribes and librarians, today's mermaids continue the work their first ancestors started, copying, safeguarding, and keeping alive every story, whether oral or written or both. Although they have modernized. Now, in addition to making hard copies on paper of all stories, the mermaids also make digital copies. Another development is that they have branched out from fiction and now transcribe written works of nonfiction as well. Remembering Homer, they handle all poetry with sweet, sentimental care.

Lest you fret the stories are ever left lonely and abandoned upon their stone shelves, I can assure you the mermaids make certain all stories get appropriate attention. Periodically, each book is pulled from its shelf and read aloud by a mermaid librarian to visiting schools of fish and groups of other sea creatures too. It makes for dynamite entertainment. The fish and other sea creatures love it.

Although it is true every copy of a story in the mermaids' library would rather be out in the world above, spoken by a human tongue, or read silently while held in human hands, they are safe and sound, free and alive in the mermaids' library. So they will remain for themselves and their companions in the sea cave deep beneath the ocean. The stories will stay put in the mermaids' library until humanity evolves to the place of wisdom where all stories are always at liberty to be told.

In the meantime, the sea elves still meet the constant demand for construction of more bookcases, as well as continue to shelve the books where the mermaids direct. The bioluminescent sea creatures still light the chambers. While the birds still deliver all stories to the mermaids, who swim out to receive them at the rocks near the shore of the sirens' old, deserted island. There the mermaids take dictation, transcribing the birds' singings into writings with waterproof ink on waterproof paper.

Regarding the birds, there is one change. Since so many stories these days are only told by way of the written word, the birds have learned to read. I would have assumed otherwise, but as luck would have it, birds are not only keen listeners, competent memorizers, and masterful singers of stories, they are also highly proficient readers.

And speaking of making assumptions, mermaids do not look the way you might assume. Especially knowing as you do the curvaceous nymphs and bewitching sirens they were made from, as well as probably seeing some splashy depictions. But the truth is, mermaid figures are as straight as love's arrow, and their chests are as flat as a sea at peace. Their hair they wear in tousled, untamed tangles, and their eyes behind thick glasses are as modest as stars in the light of day. Yet, the mermaids are every bit as alluring as their nymph and siren predecessors. They are alluring because they are boundlessly intelligent, and ever remembering their origins, they use their gift wisely with no showing off or getting led astray by their own egos.

Here's hoping you too always remember your ancestry. Of stardust and seawater, you are the miraculous stuff of always and forever. And that is true fact.

Chapter Twenty

AULD LANG SYNE

*A*S USUAL, Luna has gotten her way. Having been forcibly removed from my cabin by a pair of ruffians per her instructions, I am presently at the party the Stone Harvesters are throwing with no escape in sight. Which is annoying. Because I have so many fairytales yet to tell you. Why Luna would demand to have me interrupted now when I am finally, after all these years, keeping the promise I made her on the night we met, I do not know. I realize Luna is an unstoppable force of nature, but I nonetheless do not think it is right for a little fairy to always be bossing around a big person like myself.

What happened was, having just completed the mermaids' tale, I was getting ready to tell you a story about Pennsylvania's squonk, a fascinating magical creature who roams what is left of the state's hemlock forests. But then I heard a gentle tapping at my front door. When I answered, a chickadee flew in. It went straight for my desk and landed on the pile of fairytales I had placed there.

Chickadees are my favorite birds. Although they may not sing the catchiest songs or have the showiest feathers, they are born clowns and acrobats. Even when I am not feeling like it, chickadees make me smile. I was delighted with my unexpected guest and was thinking how lovely it would be for the two of us to spend a quiet evening together.

However, that is when Boogeyman and Baz appeared at my still open door. Totally uninvited, and with Baz having to bend his sasquatch body in half to fit through, the two trespassers invaded my home.

"Luna Shadow sent us," announced Boogeyman.

"That's right," said Baz. "We have orders to bring you, Dusty Wonders, willing or unwilling and without delay to tonight's gathering."

"But --," I started to explain.

"No excuses," cut in both buttinskies.

Next thing I knew, Boogeyman had grabbed my left arm, and Baz had grabbed my right, and, well, what else could I do but cooperate? Seriously. It is difficult and perhaps not wise as well to resist when Boogeyman and a sasquatch have you in their clutches. Not that they hurt me. But, still, I did not want to go, and on top of that, I did not like being escorted to a party

Chapter Twenty

in such an undignified fashion. My entrance was doomed to be humiliating. What would the other guests think?

"What about the bird? What about the chickadee? I can't just leave him here all alone," I pleaded as I was half-dragged and half-carried out the door.

"The bird stays where he is," answered Baz. "Don't worry, Dusty. Your chickadee will be fine. He has work to do, and I assure you, he very much enjoys his work."

I thought it a strange reply. But having lived in Lightfall Hollow among fairies and other magical creatures for so long, I am no stranger to strange. I let it go.

So here I am at the party. I must admit, I am beginning to be glad I came. So many of my dearest friends are here tonight, and they all seem to be having the time of their lives. Including Luna, who is so busy dancing she has yet to acknowledge my presence. Ha! It figures.

Even the elders are here. Father Time and Papa Space I have seen on occasion, but this is the first time I have ever laid eyes on Mother Nature. She is magnificent, tall, and powerfully built. Her skin, hair, and eyes are so black they shine with iridescence, collecting and reflecting the lights and colors of the universe so intensely it hurts to look at her.

I presume that is why she is standing off on her own, apart from the other partygoers. And now I notice the wistful look upon her face, and I can feel her aloneness. It hits me that having no equal must be the loneliest thing in the world.

Which is all the more reason for me to try to get close to her. And I do want to meet her, talk to her, get to know her. Yet, I am also afraid of her, and my instincts tell me I am right, despite feeling her pain, to keep a respectful distance between us.

However, she is irresistible. Like a moth to a flame, I am drawn to her. Only a strong hand gripping my shoulder stops me. It is Father Time. He looks down at me and gives me a stern look.

"Leave her be," says Father Time in a commanding voice. "My sister is more powerful than you can possibly know. A mere human, you would never survive a full encounter with her."

"Ain't that the truth," agrees Papa Space as he joins us.

"Now I will remind you two, this is a party," admonishes Papa Space. "Time to lighten up and have some fun. So, what's your pleasure, Dusty Wonders? Your wish is our command."

"Gosh, I don't know," I answer as I wonder why these two higher-ups are giving me the royal treatment.

"Hmm, well, a little birdie has told us that, as a little girl, you dreamed of flying like Peter Pan. Still sound good?"

"You're kidding me, right?" I try to sound gruff and disbelieving, but I can't help myself. I smile.

"Nope. We are not kidding, and you know the drill."

"Think happy things?"

"Think happy things."

I turn toward Mother Nature, our eyes meet, and without thinking, I do something rare and old-fashioned. I do a deep curtsy. I am rewarded with a slight nod of her head and the smallest of smiles.

And we are off. I am flying like Peter Pan. It is awesome, and I am seeing the entire universe. It is all quite grand, but there is not a single place I behold that feels like home the way Earth does.

"I want to go back to Earth," I shout through outer space.

"Homesick already?" ask Father Time and Papa Space in unison.

"I guess I am. Earth is a hard place to leave behind," I admit through the lump in my throat.

"Yes, indeed, Dusty Wonders. How right you are. So, let's make a few stops on your planet before we head back to the party. We're certain you'll appreciate them."

We return to Earth and travel about the globe. At home, I jump the waves of every ocean, wade every river, stream, and creek, ooh and aah at the lights of every city, town, village, and living residence, climb every mountain, hill, glacier, and dune, walk each valley, meadow, forest, and jungle, explore every cave and wilderness nook, gasp in amazement at all flora and fauna, and get down on my knees and kiss every land's dirt. I am so grateful. Because there is not a place on Earth I would not call beautiful. My heart fills and breaks at the same time.

"Time to party!" announces Papa Space.

And so here I am again. Just like that, I am back in Lightfall Hollow, and it is time to party. It is time for a good time.

I take in the friendly scene surrounding me. Although I cannot see her, I can feel the spirit of the will-o'-the-wisp ghost, Willa. She is in her element and the star of the show, telling ghost stories around the campfire. In its flames arise Ella, Izzy, Red, Blue, and Mountain, as well as Logan, unicorns, the Alleghans, and so many other dearly departed loved ones too, never to be forgotten.

Across the way, some reindeer visiting from the North Pole, along with some Pegasi visiting from heaven only knows where are giving free "pony" rides. Of course, reindeer and Pegasi are not ponies, but, then again, ponies cannot fly. So no one is complaining about the false advertising.

A leprechaun named Ciaran is directing a scavenger hunt, his pot of gold the end prize. I sure hope he knows what he is doing. While Sandman is presiding over a sand sculpture contest. I wonder how he ever got all that sand to the hollow.

Gnomes and trolls are blowing and chasing bubbles. Banshees, ogres, and goblins are playing hide and seek. Centaurs and kelpies are throwing horseshoes. Fauns are bobbing for apples, and the Minotaur is proving himself to be a commanding Simon in a game of Simon Says with the sea elves.

At the edge of Nessie's pond, Clover, Cricket, and the little green-glow alien kids are presenting Nessie with a Scottish kilt.

I suppose to apologize for the unfortunate pink goo incident. It is way too small to stay around Nessie's massive dragon-turned-lake monster waist, but she giggles when if falls off and hands it to her fairy pal, Plum.

It is way too big for tiny Plum and falls off him as well. He too giggles, and then, caught up in the generous, silly moment, the hollow resounds with the merriment of the fast friends as they toast each other with cups of lavender, rosemary, and dandelion nectar.

While the mermaids partying in Nessie's pond sing "Auld Lang Syne." Their song is haunting. It is easy for me to imagine its profound beauty floating through the hollow forever.

My chickadee swoops in. He lands in the tangled tresses of one mermaid and whistles a tune in her ear. I only catch a few notes, but the melody feels somehow familiar to me.

I look over at Baz and Boogeyman. They hold between them a long, slender stick and call for a limbo dance. The elders, along with a spider named Anansi (whose story I can hardly wait to tell you), provide the reggae music. While Mother Nature takes pity on the trees for a bit, and they line up and show how low they can go, bending backwards beneath the bar held by my two favorite, sweet and adorable brutes.

And, wow! Are the trees ever flexible! It proves to be a close competition, but with Ol-Ol cheering him on, Wilton Weeping Willow wins. Together again at last, the two lovers waltz off into the night for a private moment.

While the fairy band plays on. I'm not sure how to describe fairy music to you. It is so different, mysterious, and out-of-this-world from any music ever made by humans. All that I can tell you is, no matter how clumsy and shy you think yourself to be, you hear fairy music and know you are a dancer, and you just have to dance.

So I join my still dancing Luna Shadow. We dance our hearts out together, and it is exhilarating. But something is going on here I don't understand. I grab my trusted mentor and cherished friend by the hand and pull her aside.

"Luna, what gives? Why am I here? What's going on?"

"Well, isn't it obvious, Dusty Wonders? We're celebrating. We're celebrating our fairytales, and we're celebrating you. You've done your part, and now you're finished."

"Wait, no. First of all, I'm not done yet. You asked me to tell your fairytales, and, really, I'm just getting started. I'm not done yet."

Luna shrugs her shoulders and gives me an indifferent, I couldn't care less kind of look.

"But I'm not done yet. Hey, come on, Luna, I'm not done yet," I say as I feel my heartbeat quicken and my tummy begin to turn somersaults.

"But you are," says Luna as casually as can be. "Time to move on. Time to say good-bye."

"What? Good-bye? Are you kidding me? Is this some kind of joke?"

"No. No joke."

"So, you're serious. And this is what? My goodbye party? But, why, Luna? Why are you dumping me?"

"Oh, for goodness sake, Dusty Wonders. You know better than that. You and I are best friends forever."

"So, what then? What is it, Luna? Am I going to die soon?" I ask shakily.

"Really?" asks Luna, a droll look upon her face. "Really? Is that what you're really worried about right now? After all I've taught and shown you, after all you've learned, that's what you're really worried about right now? What a silly goose you are, Dusty Wonders!"

Then Luna grins at me with such aggravating amusement at my serious fear that I want to give her wings a vicious pull. But I don't. Because my brain is now racing a million miles a minute, and my mouth won't stop running away with it.

"Or is this going to be like in some story," I frantically continue, "where I wake up tomorrow, and I will think it has all been a dream, or worse, I will have completely forgotten everything I have loved and known and lived here?"

Luna removes the smirk on her face, lets out a big sigh, and rolls her eyes. "Dusty dear, please, I beg of you, stop with all this crazy drama. It's simply time for a change is all."

"Change? Well, who needs a change? Things are fine just the way they are."

"Dusty, you're talking like you're one of those fool giants from the Alleghan tribe, and that, my friend, is not good. Not good at all. You've done your part, and now it's time to move on, and that's that. So please stay calm and be reasonable about this."

"You say we're best friends forever, Luna, but you're still ditching me like it's nothing at all. Like I'm nothing at all."

"No! Never! But it is time to say good-bye."

"No. No. Please. Wait, wait just a minute here. This can't be good-bye. I need you, Luna. I need all of you. My friends. And I need your world. I need your magic. I can't lose you, Luna. Please don't do this to me. Please don't leave me."

"Oh, Dusty Wonders, still the same frightened child as on the night we met. Trembling in the dark, scared out of your mind to step through the open door and into the light. Just like the rest of your species. No matter how many opportunities you are given, no matter how many times it is put in front of you in black and white and every color in between, no matter how many times you write it, read it, hear it, say it, you refuse to accept responsibility for whom you are. You refuse to see that you're the magical ones."

"And while, yes, it's true my world has been around much, much longer than your world, and we have learned much, much more and progressed much, much further, you humans are the ones who can learn a whole lot more and go a whole lot further. So how it all goes from here is up to you people. Because the truth is, in this world of ours, the children are in charge."

"Well, that's really scary," I blurt out.

"Yes, it is. But there is still great reason to hope."

"Oh, yeah?" I ask in a voice loaded with gloomy disbelief. "And just why is that?"

"Because you humans are enough."

"So, come on, my dear old friend. All that remains for us now is now. So, let's make the most of it. Let's be happy now, and let's be happy together."

I am scared and sad. I sob and howl. While Luna at first makes sympathetic, and then impatient clucking sounds with her tongue. But I don't care. I think I will cry forever. However, after a while, I manage to get a hold of myself and realize Luna is right.

I see Gold, the most ancient and wisest of fairies, has started a conga line. I poke Luna in the ribs, motion my head in Gold's direction, and sniffle out a "Do you wanna dance, one last time, for old time's sake?"

Luna nods and smiles in agreement, and we join in with our friends. I grab a hold of Nessie's tail, and Luna grabs a hold of my butt. We dance the night away, and we are happy

When our dance is finished, I say the only and truest thing left to say.

"I love you, Luna Shadow."

"I love you too, Dusty Wonders."

She blows me a kiss, turns, and flies away.

Chapter Twenty-One

THE NEW DAY

*D*AWN IS breaking, and suddenly I am so tired I can think only of bed and sleep. I leave the party and head back to my cabin without even saying good-bye to my friends. But I know they will understand. After all, I have done my part.

On my way, I pass a young boy. He appears to be about eight years old. By the curious look on his face, it is obvious he can hear the party's otherworldly music and is drawn to it.

I recognize this boy. I believe his name is Pete, the same as my father's was. He is the son of the British couple who purchased property and built a new home about a mile up the road. A while back they moved in. I am no longer Lightfall Hollow's only human resident.

The boy has taken to wandering the woods, usually with a big, scruffy St. Bernard at his heels and a crow upon his shoulder. We have bumped into each other on several occasions. Although we never say more than hello, I look into the boy's eyes, and it is clear he sees magic is present, alive, and well in Lightfall Hollow. Like me and my father, he is wonderstruck.

At present, I am concerned for the child. His two loyal companions are absent this morning. The boy is all alone in the woods when it is yet not fully light. I see he is trembling. He is afraid. Perhaps I should stop him and escort him back to his parents. But I am so tired, and besides, when Luna sees him, I know she will take him under her wing. There is nothing to worry about.

That settled, I continue home. I reach the cabin as a white moon is setting and a red sun is rising. I am still thinking of how beautiful the world is as I crawl into bed. Curling up under the soft, warm covers, I feel contented and safe. A few moments later, I fall peacefully asleep.

I dream I am a little girl again. I am riding on my father's shoulders through an enchanted forest. The moose, George, ambles alongside us, gloriously tossing his perfect antlers towards the heavens. His thick, deep brown fur gleams, and his bright eyes sparkle mischievously. Unable to resist such a noble beast, I lean over and give him a little kiss on one of his velvety ears. He smells of spring and green, growing things.

During our journey, we cross paths with countless magical creatures. Daddy knows them all. He greets each one by name.

The magical creatures call him by name too. It is not the name I recognize as my father's, but it is a name I know.

Although I never would guessed it. Yet, the name rings true. And I finally understand what my father, mother, and Luna always understood.

I am my father's daughter.

The End

ACKNOWLEDGEMENTS

The Fairytales of Lightfall Hollow has its origin in someone I never met. William Charles Mountain was my maternal grandfather. An immigrant from England, he died twenty years before I was born.

Although a consummate woodsman, masterful gardener, and philosophical thinker, my grandfather was poor, lacking in formal education, and he could not read. Be that as it may, he caught the feminine catch of the Pennsylvania community where he had settled. Susan Ellen Frew was an American of Scotch and Irish descent. While poor too, she was no stranger to masculine wooing. She had already rejected a long line of suitors by the time William proposed and she said yes.

Susan's affirmative answer to William's question did not sit well with her other male admirers. They were outraged that the woman of their dreams had fallen, not for a prosperous home-boy, but for a penniless foreigner. It was too much to bear. So, one dark night, several of them ganged up and attacked William as he was walking his sweetheart home.

Yet, according to family lore, despite being largely outnumbered during the fistfight, the only significant injury William suffered was a cracked rib when Susan jumped into the fray, missed her target, and accidentally kicked her betrothed with one of her high button boots.

Shortly thereafter, when the rib had healed, the couple married. They remained poor throughout their marriage, and they suffered many hardships, including, among the seven children born to them, the death of a baby girl, Beatrice, and the death of a little boy, Wilbur. Still, overall, they were happy.

This is true even though there was an occasion when William did something that could be considered entirely foolish. He took the money he and Susan had been pragmatically saving for some necessities and used it to purchase all twelve volumes of Nora Alleyne and Andrew Lang's collected fairytales, *Andrew Lang's Fairy Books of Many Colors*. This from a man of humble means who could not read. I can only imagine what my grandmother's initial reaction must have been.

However, she must have eventually come around. Because Susan could read, and she read the fairy books to her husband and children. One of those children was my mother.

Although the fairy books, like my grandfather, were long gone from our family by the time I was a child, my mother remembered them with great fondness, and, as best as her memory could serve her, she would sometimes recount to me several of the fairytales in the collection.

The fairytales found in this book are very different from the fairytales my grandfather brought home to his wife and children, but I am confident that Nora Alleyne and Andrew Lang's fairy books are in the ancestry of my fairytales and my ancestry too. Along with someone I never met.

For I have not a doubt my grandfather has influenced my life and that we are forever bonded in a close relationship. Within our common ground, *The Fairytales of Lightfall Hollow* took root. And, for that, I acknowledge and thank William Charles Mountain.

I owe much thanks and acknowledgement as well to my editor, Robin Moore. Robin, as a renowned writer of stories and professional storyteller in the oral tradition, has given of himself and to the world some of the best stories I have ever had the privilege to experience, several of which will stay with me forever. I highly recommend Robin's stories to all readers and listeners. If you have not already read Robin Moore's stories or heard them spoken aloud, give yourself the opportunity to read and/or hear them. And, if you already know his stories, give yourself the further benefit to read and/or hear them again. Robin Moore's stories are timeless.

As for me, I could not have written *The Fairytales of Lightfall Hollow* without Robin's help. His guidance was always right on the mark. The best parts of the fairytales are outcomes of suggestions he made. In addition, he was ever accessible, ever patient, and ever encouraging, and he always talked to me in a manner that was down-to-earth, respectful, considerate, and friendly.

While, at the same time, he sagely offered me challenges that improved my writing.

Then there is the fact that Robin has expertise in so many areas. He not only knows writing and how to prompt a writer to write to the best of their ability, he also knows the industry and all the ins and outs of self-publishing. He saved me so much time, energy, and frustration with the support he provided with his technical savvy.

In short, every writer should be so lucky as to have as their editor, Robin Moore.

I am also thankful for my illustrator, Kathy Hebner. Like Robin, she was such a pleasure and so easy to work with. She consulted with me, listened to me, and generously allowed me a good amount of input as she created her art, as well as kept me informed about her progress. She graciously accepted all my comments and always maintained a can-do attitude throughout our partnership. Not to mention how quickly and diligently she worked.

Best of all, Kathy's finished illustrations exceeded my already high expectations. She successfully captured with paint and canvas the whimsical characters and scenes I had imagined and tried to write about in the fairytales. While her art for the book's cover is the perfect depiction of the overriding wonder, hope, and joy I tried to convey throughout the fairytales. I am truly sorry for Kathy and my collaboration to come to an end. It has been both meaningful and fun.

ACKNOWLEDGEMENTS

No writer has ever had a more supportive spouse than I. My husband, Richard, has stuck with me through the entire writing process, painstakingly reading my each and every draft, while somehow always finding something positive to say about my latest, sometimes worthless attempt at worthily telling a worthy story. He is my first, most loyal, and best reader. Although it was my grandfather who helped the fairytales to take root, it was Richard who helped them to grow and blossom.

Among Richard's many talents is a knack for invention. Originally, Lightfall was a name he created for one of his inventions, and then it also became the name of the home he designed and built and where he and his wife raised their children. Many years later, Lightfall continued its evolvement, becoming for me the perfect name to capture how the first fairies came to be, as well as the perfect name for the little valley where they came to be.

I also owe a debt of gratitude to my son, Wes. A creative thinker and diligent seeker of knowledge and truth, as well as the wisest, funniest, most compassionate, selfless, courageous, and extraordinary person any mother ever had the honor to call her kid, he is my best teacher and the person I wish most to emulate. Moreover, he knows how to make me laugh.

When Wes was a little boy, I read to him. I read to him all the time. But sometimes he would ask me to tell him one of my own stories. But I would always clam up. My mind would go blank, and my heart would tighten. Well, now at last I am opening up and telling my stories. They are not to or for my child, but rather because of him.

Finally, I would like to thank all the people in my life who have told me I have a gift for writing and that I should at least try to more generously share my gift. Your kind encouragement and sweet badgering worked. I am so blessed. I am so grateful.

ABOUT THE AUTHOR

Susan C. Ramirez grew up in a working-class family in the Allegheny Mountains of Pennsylvania. Her family could not afford to buy a house, so they rented one half of an ordinary suburban duplex. But what they did have as theirs, at least in part, was the woodland hollow with its extraordinary cabin Susan describes in *The Fairytales of Lightfall Hollow*. It was there Susan as a young girl first fell under  the magnetic spell of Mother Nature and her awesome magic.

Yet, when Susan became an adult, she had to earn her keep. This reality compelled her to move to Washington, D.C. where she consecutively managed two committees of the U.S. Senate and directed the National Women's Political Caucus. After that, because by then she was among the way too few financially privileged with choices, Susan chose to be a stay-at-home mom, a wonderful gig that lasted seventeen years.

During all her many fantastic adventures throughout that long time, Susan never stopped imagining she would someday come home to the hollow. And finally, she did.

Now Susan lives there. Her current cabin is a quaint and cozy little house full of peculiarities, imperfections, and memories that give the modest home an air of true enchantment. Sharing the same captivating abode are Susan's loving husband, a charmer of a dog named Ember, and an imp of a cat named Pia.

As for Mother Nature, she is still in the hollow, gracing Susan's life with her awesome magic. As she graces your life anywhere on the good Earth you happen to be.

You can visit Susan at www.susancramirez.com.

ABOUT THE ILLUSTRATOR

Nestled in the woodlands of rural Pennsylvania you will find the studio of Kathy Hebner, a self-taught artist inspired by nature and driven by empathy.

Kathy started her art career in 1990 with her father. The two of them founded a craft show business, rightly named "Just Me & My Dad."

Since her father's passing, Kathy has carried on, utilizing different mediums, often using antique windows and doors as her canvases. She also gathers seashells and transforms them into works of art.

Her artwork can be found in boutiques and fine gift shops throughout the country.

In *The Fairytales of Lightfall Hollow*, Kathy's whimsical,

unique, and highly expressive illustrations visually interact with the reader and set the tone for each story. Additionally, the book's cover illustration evinces Kathy's extraordinary sense of color. All clearly reflect Kathy's love of the natural world and her empathy for all of creation.

AUTHOR'S NOTE

If you have read *The Fairytales of Lightfall Hollow*, I would sincerely appreciate your writing a review of the book. Reviews are particularly important to me as an author because I hope to do more writing in the future, and I want to become as good a writer as I possibly can. To do so, I need the helpful comments of my readers.

To write a review, go to the Amazon listing for this book, which you can find by searching Amazon for its title or through my author page at www.amazon.com/author/susancramirez and scrolling down to "Customer Reviews." There, click on "Write a customer review."

Thank you so much for your consideration.

Made in the USA
Middletown, DE
16 March 2024

50965781R00117